Duchess in Danger

Trisha Dann

Best wishes from Trisha Dann

Copyright © 2016 Trisha Dann

All rights reserved.

ISBN: 13:97815306236600
ISBN-10:153062360X:

Trisha Dann

"THIS, THEN, IS A SOURCE OF OUR DESIRE TO LOVE EACH OTHER. LOVE IS BORN INTO EVERY HUMAN BEING: IT CALLS BACK THE HALVES OF OUR ORIGINAL NATURE TOGETHER; IT TRIES TO MAKE ONE OUT OF TWO AND HEAL THE WOUND OF HUMAN NATURE."

PLATO

I THANK MY BEAUTIFUL GRANDAUGHTER, COURTNEY, FOR DESIGNING MY BOOK COVER.

ALSO, MY HUSBAND, DAVID FOR HIS PATIENCE WHILE I TRAVELLED BACK INTO THE REGENCY PERIOD.

SPECIAL THANKS TO MY LOVELY DAUGHTER, SONYA FOR HER EXCELLENT ADVICE.

THANK YOU TO MY TWO HANDSOME SONS AND MY DAUGHTER IN LAW, WHO ENCOURAGED ME TO, 'GO FOR IT!'.

CONTENTS

Prologue	6
Chapter One	34
Chapter Two	53
Chapter Three	74
Chapter Four	90
Chapter Five	112
Chapter Six	130
Chapter Seven	146
Chapter Eight	156
Chapter Nine	177
Chapter Ten	197
Chapter Eleven	218
Chapter Twelve	237
Chapter Thirteen	256
Chapter Fourteen	272
Chapter Fifteen	285
Chapter Sixteen	297
Chapter Seventeen	317
Epilogue	327

Duchess in Danger

Prologue

𝓕or months afterwards, the Charity Benevolent Fundraiser was rated an unequivocal success by both the local gentry and lesser inhabitants of the small town of Muchbury, which nestled in the County of Somerset.

For Reverend Jonas Althrop, in a moment of pure inspiration, after a conversation with a young lady of noble birth, had formed the excellent notion of raising funds for a new orphanage.

For the most part, he had no more expectation than it would achieve the grand sum of fifty pounds. However, he was pleasantly surprised, and for many years afterwards, congratulated himself on his achievement.

If he had not been so puffed up in his own consequence he would have owned that a certain young lady of noble birth deserved the praise far more than he did. Left to his own devices, the reverend's invitations would have been restricted to local gentry, whose numbers were very few at that time of year. The reason of course for the depletion in the town's population, was that many resided in London during the Little Season.

It was the youthful, Lady Arabella, who, at the tender age of sixteen, anticipated that if matters remained as they were, the event would culminate in nothing but a slow afternoon. This lady didn't allow grass to grow under her feet and threw herself into assisting the reverend in his worthy cause. As the only child of an Earl, she had a passion for worthwhile causes much to her parents' displeasure.

After much pondering over how she could achieve a successful outcome, she had decided to write to her many friends and acquaintances who lived further afield.

Triumph was largely due to the invitations she had sent, which had been laboriously written and promptly accepted. Her dedication to the cause and her popularity boded well for a lively afternoon's entertainment. Those who wished to purchase a ticket for Muchbury Assembly Rooms at an astronomical sum, would receive an extremely select evening of dance and cards.

At this time of the year, for many waiting for the London Season to begin, life was not overly exciting, so she believed that something out of the ordinary would offer those hankering after a little pleasure, an opportunity to relieve the tedium. Lady Arabella had invited her friends from Miss Jenkins Academy for Young Ladies, where she had resided in Gloucestershire for three long years.

As an extremely popular student of that Academy, success was assured, as the school only accepted the highest nobility in the land. She had assumed quite rightly as it turned out, that many of the young ladies would be accompanied by their fond parents. Some would persuade their brothers and their friends, who would help to elevate the numbers.

Thinking back to that eventful day, even the sunshine had remained in its proper place, bathing the square with warm approval.

The afternoon was a huge success with everyone in high spirits, enjoying the various entertainments. Jovial voices were to be heard laughing and greeting one another across the square. For those of a competitive nature there was the archery contest and for others, who wished to sit in the warm, hazy, afternoon sunshine, refreshments were offered at an enhanced price. Those gentlemen who wished to partake of refreshments from the local Inn were obliged for this day only, to pay an entrance fee every time they made a purchase.

This was such a unique idea amongst the more affluent visitors, it became a joke to pay the enormous sums to enter the building, particularly so after a few drinks.

For once, everyone was behaving admirably and Arabella was thrilled with the profits from the afternoon.

She prayed that the evening would be as successful. They were to set out from her aunt's house as her parents were visiting London. She thought about her mama and papa as they sat in the carriage. Mama would be enjoying a gossip with her friends, while Papa would be visiting his mistress.

She knew that young ladies should not be aware of such things, but Molly, her maid often gossiped to her friend in the hallway and Arabella had overheard an interesting conversation one evening when they were unaware that she was inside her bedroom. As they were talking outside her room, it was nothing to press her ear against the door and learn all about her father's less than secret liaisons with his mistresses. Apparently, there had been many during the last few years and most of the servants knew about them.

After what seemed an age, she was finally sitting with her aunt, at the farthest end of the Assembly Rooms. A feeling of nervous anticipation flooded her body as she hoped that everyone she had invited would attend. Luckily, she was not to be disappointed and for a long time afterwards, the local gentry spoke about it as a sad crush where everyone who was anyone had elected to be present.

For the small town, it became a fond memory that entertained many in local drawing rooms during morning calls. Reverend Althrop, who was happy to accept all the credit, was elevated amongst his wealthy parishioners as a great gun. From that evening onwards, he was invited to drawing rooms where those who enjoyed their select gatherings had once ignored his presence completely.

Even those who lived in poverty found a good word to say about him.

"Perhaps he weren't as bad as he always seemed," old man Jarvis was heard to say.

This was a surprise to say the least, as it was generally known that the reverend had never done anything other than denounce the poor amongst his congregation as sinners, frequently warning them about the hell that they all deserved.

It had been decided that a proportion of the money would be placed to one side to ensure that the rooves of the old cottages on Sir Hilary Farthindale's Estate were mended, providing his tenants with some measure of warmth. Having lost most of his money at cards, he had nothing left to assist them and they were forced to live in abject poverty. This gentleman was not overly concerned about them, however and being of a happy go lucky frame of mind, was anticipating the coming London Season as a time to recoup his losses if he was not successful beforehand.

At present, this noteworthy young man lounged against the wall in the Assembly Rooms, scanning the crowds for likely victims who might save him the expense and inconvenience of a visit to town. His main concern this evening as he surveyed the crowd was to leave at the end of the evening more warm in the pocket than he had arrived. A confident man, he believed there were two ways that he could accomplish this aspiration.

He could fleece some unsuspecting young greenhorn at the card table or target some unassuming heiress who was hanging out for an old, respectable title.

Coming into his inheritance at a very young age had dealt him no favours. After successfully seducing almost half the maids in his employ, (the others inspiring no hint of desire within him), he used his dark good looks and charming manner to attain whatever and whomever took his fancy. As a young, vibrant man with a taste for wine, women and cards, he believed he was a prime catch.

Meanwhile, Reverend Althrop was deliriously happy as he surveyed the gentry present on that particular evening. As the third son of a Baron, the Reverend Jonas Althrop believed he belonged in such exalted company and as he was presently hanging out for a rich wife, looked around with interest at the many ladies present.

Many years earlier, he had lost his heart to a young lady whose father had strongly disapproved of a match between them. He had never forgotten her and how speedily her father had married her off to an old crony with the requisite wealth and title.

Recently he had heard that she had become a widow, but the reverend was too proud to pursue that lady again. Now, he looked more closely to home to find a quiet young woman of good family who might possess a decent enough dowry to ensure him a large stable of hunters. Obsessed with his own consequence, he had even thought about Lady Arabella as a prime target for his aspirations, but he was aware that the Earl was a somewhat stuffy individual and would look much higher for an alliance for his only child.

Pity! he mused, *She is young enough to mould to my liking!*

For a while he continued to ponder over Lady Arabella and then a decided frown marred his somewhat craggy features.

Lately, he had noticed a certain stubbornness in the lady's character that was to be deplored. Even though she was very young, she had shown herself to be somewhat headstrong and would be difficult to guide into the correct behaviour he desired in a woman.

She was also rather a tall lady and he had a preference for small, delicate women who would know their place in the order of things. Someone like his old flame, his lost love, Henrietta.

There were a number of rich widows in the neighbourhood who would suit his temperament. Lately, he had been growing a little impatient, however, as he had his eye on a prime hunter that was a little out of his monetary reach. He would need to give the matter of his nuptials much more attention. Looking around him, he decided that this event was a gift from heaven. The poverty around him in the village did not interest him one bit. His sense of consequence did. Even the Bible said that the poor would be with us till the end of time! Who was he, a more affluent, privileged person to argue or change the order of things!

No, he thought; *The poor had their place in society and must not forget it.*

Suddenly, he became aware of Lady Peters, a widow whom he knew hung on every word uttered in his Sunday sermons. Admittedly, she was much older than he would have liked, but rumour had it that she had been left a goodly fortune by her late husband. She was just out of her widow weeds and looking quite fetching in her violet, silk gown.

It might be worth cosying up to her.

At this very moment, she was smiling across at him. *Why not?* he thought and marched over to what would become in a hideously short amount of time, his future wife.

****

His tall frame would command attention anywhere, but in Muchbury Assembly Rooms, his presence shone out like an overly bright beacon, which in turn, caused more than one matron to urge her protégé to sit up to show themselves to advantage. Many a heart fluttered as he sauntered around the stuffy, over-crowded room where the local populace stared in a state of both curiosity and anticipation. As a charismatic figure, the young ladies pruned and preened and simpered, trying their utmost to gain his attention. Unfortunately, he seemed unaware of their existence.

He was by no means alone, accompanied by a group of friends, but for some reason, there was some indefinable reason that he stood out from the crowd.

An old lady, sitting with the rest of the dowagers was pushed to remark to her friend of some standing, that he carried a certain sense of authority; instilled with a confidence that could only come from his striking, good looks and considerable wealth.

"That tailor of his knows his business!" the old lady remarked. She sniffed, shaking her head, knowingly, risking her purple turban that was a little on the large side. It slid to the side of her head and she managed to pause its descent to the floor by a hair's breath.

"His fine coat fits him like a second skin," she continued.

Her friend following the progress of the group of males pointed out excitedly,

"And only look at those chiselled features! My dear, if I was only twenty years younger I declare I would swoon at his feet." The lady used her fan vigorously, overcome by her heated thoughts.

It was not every day that such a bunch of virile men visited this neck of the woods. The thought hovered on many a fond parent's mind that this was a rare opportunity indeed to be honoured with a visit from so many illustrious young men who might find themselves attracted to at least one of their offspring.

If any one of them became interested and a serious courtship ensued, it would certainly save the expense of a Season in town. Some of the fond mamas could be forgiven for their frugal thoughts, especially those with more than one young lady to launch into society.

The gentlemen appeared to be the guests of the young Lord Walter Murray, who had recently married the only daughter of a wealthy Cit, much to the condemnation of local society. This undoubtedly created problems, as no-one present had acknowledged Lady Murray up until this moment. Here was a dilemma! If they were to make any headway with the illustrious gentlemen, they would be forced to greet Lady Murray or risk censure and disapproval from her guests. Furthermore, if Lord and Lady Murray mingled with the likes of rich bachelors, then it would behove every aspiring mama to make haste to welcome her to their circle.

Not everyone was in awe of the virile young men, however.

"They look a rum lot by all accounts," Lady Silvester was heard to say in the voice of one who suffered prodigiously with a deafness that was the bane of her young niece.

That young niece was at present, noticeably cringing as she realised that the gentlemen could hear every word between a break in the music.

"I see they are with Lord Murray and the Cit! Very bad ton to be sure!"

"Aunt Maria, please……….. I do so wish you would keep your voice down." Arabella frantically whispered as all eyes were drawn to the old, formidable lady.

Lady Silvester turned to her niece, a look of disapproval prominent on her face.

"Now I won't have any of your missish ways here Arabella, let me tell you. Most people, if they are honest would agree with me."

Her niece merely cringed as heads turned and leaned forward to listen to the old lady, more clearly.

"Everyone knows that I don't dress things up in fancy linen," she continued, oblivious to the stares she was receiving from those closest to her. Moving slightly to settle her over abundant form on the sofa, she sniffed and adopted an air of disapproval as her eyes followed various inhabitants of the room.

No one who knew Lady Silvester well could accuse her of labouring a point. Her conversation was often blatantly disrespectful towards those she barely tolerated but once she issued a point of view, she would move on rapidly to her next victim.

"I see Henrietta Winterbourne has that vulgar yellow concoction on again. Her face is far too sallow for that colour. Her mother never did have much style."

She continued to speak in her raised voice, unaware that her niece had her eyes fixed rigidly on the floor attempting to decrease herself in size as the old lady castigated all those whom she felt offended her dignity.

Arabella was well used to her aunt's disapproval of those around her, but her embarrassment knew no bounds at that precise moment.

Meanwhile, the group of young blades, moved around the room, laughingly sharing much banter.

"Hey Walter," A tall dark gentleman said. "I've decided to offer you first refusal on my high steppers! My tailor's pressing for settlement and father will not finance me till next quarter day."

"I'll have em," Lord Murray replied, rubbing his hands together. "By jove, you beat me to them last year at

Tatts. I knew at the time I would have them sooner or later."

"Ain't the heiress you was after come up to scratch?" Perry asked.

"Afraid not, her father won't hear of the match. Hanging out for a Duke no less! Someone like Seb's brother!" James replied wryly, looking cast down.

"Or Seb," Lord Murray stated, "He's already inherited lands, title and wealth from his mother's side of the family. He must be one of the wealthiest men in the kingdom."

"Gentlemen, gentlemen," Lord Darcy Rutherford admonished, tedium emanating from his lithe body that was for once masked by an ungainly slouch.

"Must you make a humdrum evening even more tiresome by wrangling over wealth?"

Chastised by this noted nonpareil, they swiftly changed the subject. It did not do to offend Darcy or Seb. They were there to be emulated. Almost instantly, the young men's interest transferred to the day's hunting.

"I say, Darcy, that showy hunter you rode today! Was he one of Seb's?" James asked with a note of respect in his voice.

"No, Gold Fire is my own mount and he's not for sale before you ask it. He's one of the best hunters I've had."

"None of us could afford him, anyhow!" Perry stated. They all agreed then returned to the capers of the day, still oblivious to the lures and feminine sighs that followed them as they continued to roast one another.

While his friends discussed hunters, the dark Adonis, stood slightly apart from the general throng casting his eyes over the scene before him observing various antics of the young ladies present in some amusement until he settled on a mouse of a girl. She was the only one that he could see who appeared disinterested in the new arrivals.

Earlier, he had heard the lady who was possibly her

mother, speaking her mind.

Obviously, an eccentric and well used to holding her own, he thought.

Now, glancing at the young lady, he rather felt sorry for her. Dressed as she was, she would never cut a dash like the other young ladies in the room, yet something in her dark eyes that almost looked too large for her face, intrigued him.

Suddenly, he realised he was guilty of staring blatantly at her, much to the young lady's discomfort. As his friends tried to roast him, he ignored them completely, his concentration remaining on the one young lady, who was now very much aware of his scrutiny. She was blushing profusely in a very pretty manner at his singular behaviour. He really should have pity on her, but there was something about her that intrigued him.

"Arabella, will you fetch me a lemonade?" the redoubtable old lady asked. "I swear I will faint from the heat in here unless I have something to cool me down.

It really is too much, especially when one is forced to endure the presence of strangers whom we don't know from Adam."

The old lady had recourse to her handkerchief and blew her nose in a way that attracted attention from those who sat close to her.

"You know I don't like riff raff and one can't tell these days whom one is rubbing shoulders with, but I do try to hold myself up and not succumb to the megrims like your dear mother. This is just the type of entertainment she would abhor."

Arabella stood as quickly as it was seemly to do to prevent her aunt expanding on her theme.

A lemonade might take her mind off the strangers in the room.

"Yes, Aunt Maria, Pray don't tease yourself so. You will bring on one of your spasms," she replied, conscious of a steely gaze piercing her skin and really beginning to feel quite resentful of such ill manners whether it was those of her aunt or the very dark Adonis.

With her dear, old aunt, her testiness was natural, as she had lately been diagnosed with a heart complaint. The poor dear was tetchy at the best of times. There was no excuse for the tall, dark stranger. His manners were deplorable! She surreptitiously glanced at the gentleman who to her dismay was still acting rather singular, staring at her in that way that made her feel quite tingly inside. To make matters worse, she knew an unbecoming blush was creeping up her face and she could feel herself perspiring.

It was a relief to remove herself out of his line of vision. Now, he had made her quite angry.

How dare the man stare at me in this rude fashion!

Her head tilted up a notch as she concentrated upon moving through the guests, smiling at many and greeting others. As she chatted amiably with one of her friends from the Academy she had spent so many years in, she was able to regain her composure and found herself relaxing and enjoying herself once more.

Eventually, she reached the refreshments laid out on a table in the far corner of the room.

It was as she procured the lemonade for her aunt, that she became conscious of a figure breathing down her neck. Her body responded by considerably stiffening as she slowly turned to discover a gentleman deep in his cups, swaying towards her. His face portrayed a look she could not like.

He was tall and towered over her as she attempted to pass him to return to her aunt. When she moved to the left of him, he had the gall to mirror her footsteps, all the time, leering at her; the lecherous look in his eyes beginning to frighten her. She arched her eyebrows and stared angrily up. A chill rose up her spine. His face held an evil look that made her wish to cringe away.

"Well, what have we here?" he sneered, aware of the way she tried to escape his company. He stiffened, masking annoyance that she should dare to rebuff him, he moved closer to her body seemingly enjoying her discomfort. She responded with a frown and pierced the man with a cold stare.

"Please sir, kindly move so that I may pass," now a little frightened by his heated gaze.

He ignored her shaky plea.

"Stay awhile, if you please, my beauty," he slurred as she tried in vain to extricate herself.

"Please sir, I must return to my aunt." He ignored her completely and swayed towards her with what she thought was a stupid smirk on his face. Obviously, he was enjoying her discomfort.

"Take a turn around the terrace," he whispered, perilously close to her ear. She could feel his breath brushing her cheeks and started to tremble.

"I'll put a smile on your face." He sneered at a seemingly secret joke and continued to sway overly close to her. Their bodies were almost touching and Arabella started to feel really terrified. It was so unseemly and if anyone should notice, they would probably blame her for being too forward.

She remembered her mother's warnings about situations such as this. Society always found fault with the lady. It would be said that she had encouraged him with her coming ways. Hopefully, no-one could hear the conversation.

"The lady has expressed a desire to return to her aunt." A quiet voice stated in a no nonsense tone.

Totally ignoring everyone else around him, the man lurched even further and placed his hand on her shoulder to steady himself. She instantly moved backwards until she felt the table of refreshments shake behind her.

"The lady has asked you to move! If you were a gentleman you would do so at once!" the strong but quiet voice insisted.

The drunken man frowned, becoming aware that someone was addressing him. The man turned to the voice and in sudden recognition, his face contorted into another ugly sneer. He appeared to sober at once, saying,

"Well, if it ain't, Sebastian!"

He stumbled towards him and grinned in a vile way, but the gentleman stood his ground calmly. They were roughly the same size yet the air of authority that emanated from Sebastian, appeared to add height. Although, the man lurched drunkenly, rocking slowly backwards and forwards, he still remained coherent. "You would not believe with your haughty ways that we have much in common. But one day, to be sure, you will rue the day you looked down your nose at me. How dare you question whether I am a gentleman!"

"Sir, I do not think we have ever met. Just leave the lady alone," Sebastian answered in a cold tone. He was slightly confused, while he studied the drunk. Although his features looked familiar, he could not place him.

"You've been warned!" The man sniggered and slowly ambled away. Turning back towards them, he suddenly warned,

"Take heed, you'll rue this night's work!"

After he had gone, Lady Arabella sighed thankfully. She turned to her Adonis and thanked him feeling so thankful for his timely intervention. She would be eternally grateful to him for rescuing her from such a distasteful scene.

She had always imagined an Adonis to be fair, but this man's face framed by jet black hair, held so much beauty, Aphrodite and Persephone could be forgiven for falling for him. She scanned the room to see if the drunk had left the building. Thankfully, there was no sign of him.

"I don't know who he is and I am sure he didn't receive an invitation from me. He appeared to know who you were, though." She queried, glancing shyly up into his face.

Those eyes! A vivid blue, they held so much mirth and were mesmerising. A sigh escaped her. *I would never be Aphrodite in his eyes!*

"I cannot say that I know him," he replied, oblivious to the young lady's thoughts. "Yet his face looks oddly familiar." For a few seconds, a frown marred his perfect face.

He glanced after the gentleman who had disappeared through the crowd. He shook his head from side to side.

"Probably heard my friends call me by name and resents my interference or has mistaken my identity for someone he holds a grudge against."

For a while, his thoughts appeared transfixed by the drunk. He could not place him, yet his face looked so very familiar. This confused him. Presently, becoming aware once more of the young lady next to him a gentle smile stole over his face.

"Too much to drink I'm afraid." He said ruefully, "he has not caused you any harm, I trust?" showing a touching concern.

"She shook her head, smiling. I'm fine, thank you, sir! It was a little frightening for me for a while, but your kindly intervention had me recovering in a trice."

A smile of relief creased his face.

"Then I will return to my friends with your leave." He answered.

Arabella curtseyed and after he bowed to her, he moved away leaving her feeling quite bereft. As she returned to her aunt, she thankfully realised that he was talking to one of his associates. Both men laughed, after looking her way.

Were they laughing at me?

A blush crept up from her throat to the top of her head, as unwanted and unfamiliar feelings pervaded her being.

For a moment she was back in her Papa's study, listening to his scathing words and his bitter disappointment in producing a useless daughter instead of a fine son who could inherit his vast lands. She always felt vulnerable and weak in front of a father who could not love her and who used every moment in her company to disparage her. She shook her head as if to dispel the unwanted memories of an unhappy childhood.

Surely, everyone has a right to feel valued?

She hoped they were not laughing at her. Once again, she started to feel insignificant.

Damn her Papa.

Recollecting herself and where she was, once again she became conscious of her dark Adonis turning towards the card room, set up for the privileged number who found the games more to their liking than the country dances in the main hall. She was grateful to him for coming to her aid so promptly and again wondered why he had stared at her in the beginning. She knew she was nothing to look at. In the eyes of many she was still a schoolroom miss. Her papa had told her that often enough. Then she remembered how her aunt had voiced such loud, negative opinions about the newcomers.

In a way, she was thankful that he had decided to exit the room and enjoy a game of cards with his friends. Ironically, a part of her wanted to call him back so that she could explain how Aunt Maria didn't mean to be so personal. That it was just her way of talking. The poor dear had little enough happiness in her life, but common sense returned. He would forget about her after a few minutes. He would not be interested in anything she had to say, as he was probably used to the beauties of the London Season. No doubt he would think her a real milk and water miss compared to them.

She was well aware that her clothes were decidedly old fashioned. Arabella had always resisted her mama's regular offers of a new wardrobe. There were numerous poor people in the town that could eat for a year on the amount her mama thought appropriate to pay for gowns. She rarely went out in company so did not feel the need to spend money on vanity, much to her mama's dismay.

"When you have your London Season, you will wear only the finest of clothes, my dear and with none of these die away airs you are so want to display," her mother would say.

The next morning, sitting in the blue room once again at home, her mind drifted back to the handsome young man who would probably become a distant memory as time went by. She remembered how his vivid blue eyes had narrowed as he had stared intently at her. Looking back, his demeanour had been somewhat forbidding but when she considered the raised voice of her aunt, she could see that it was only natural that he would be offended by her words. After all, he did not know her forthright ways. Her aunt's bark was always worse than her bite.

She wondered if he had thought he might know her, such had been the intensity of his gaze. A blush bathed her face as she remembered the marked attention she had received and wondered if anyone else had noticed it.

He had rescued her from an embarrassing situation and she would be forever grateful towards him. She could have been ruined even before she had her first Season. How she wished her mama had attended instead of Aunt Maria, but mama was in London probably enjoying a comfortable gossip with her friends, while her father enjoyed his mistress's attentions. She instantly felt ashamed of her thoughts.

It had been kind of her aunt to chaperone her. At the tender age of sixteen, she was still not out, so was grateful that her aunt had accompanied her.

I hope, I might see the handsome Adonis again when I have my Season.

In any event, she would weave dreams around his person for the next few months, until she reached London. Little did she suspect that more than four years would pass before she met him face to face once more.

Chapter One

Four years later

"My dear Sebastian," Lady Constance Peabody implored, you owe it to the family. It is high time you applied yourself to your duty."

She took a deep breath and searched his face for evidence of the slightest response to her words, then added,

"You know I am right in this."

Her shoulders stiffened distinctly as she took in a slow, deep breath but she saw no evidence of the slightest riposte and became even more incensed. Her Ladyship stared at her recalcitrant nephew determined to make her point. Twitching her blue bombazine skirts; (a habit she was inclined to indulge when somewhat annoyed), she leant forward more firmly on her cane and peered closely through her looking glass at her nephew's tall, broad frame.

His stiff, unbending stance was evidence of his Grace's present mood as he stood by the window and purposely turned to present his back to his elderly relative. It was a grey, damp, foggy day which he felt reflected his disposition admirably. January could be such a bleak, depressing month. Murky, miserable days and long, drawn out nights did nothing to alleviate the dark moods which regularly engulfed him. Isolation and emptiness. They were his constant bedfellows.

He had travelled to London as the Parliamentary sessions opened, but longed to return to the country. It was the one place he felt at peace or as near to it as he was likely to experience, given the recent events that he was presently forced to deal with.

After what seemed an age, but was in fact a few, silent moments his reaction was a snort of sheer disgust. His life was never his own these days. He thought of his aunt's words. Every muscle in his body went rigid as he considered them. Anger rose like bile in his throat. He would need to stay calm. No-one dared to question his behaviour, except for this woman now sitting in his own morning room, having the gall to lecture him. He stiffened. He wore his arrogant stance, lofty manner and almost sinister aura like armour that exuded an impenetrable barrier to those who dared attempt to breach the defence mechanisms he had steadily built during the last two years.

Heaving a deep sigh, he slowly turned from his perusal of the cold, damp wilderness outside and his piercing, blue eyes speared her as he barked,

"I will be the judge of what is owed to my family and I'll thank you to remember it."

Many would have shrank from the mere look he bestowed upon his erstwhile relative, but his wily aunt was made of sterner stuff and was determined to make him understand the import of this meeting she had forced upon him. Determined to say her piece and jolt him out of his self-imposed melancholy which she feared threatened his very existence, she decided that attack was the only way to penetrate his defence.

"I do so wish you would climb down from that high horse and listen to some common sense. This melancholia you have adopted over the last year is coming it a bit too strong," she stated, pointing her finger toward him.

"Furthermore, young man, it is high time you pulled yourself out of the sulks and thanked heaven for what you have. You have the responsibility for the future of the dukedom and its vast estates to consider. Too many people rely on you for you to continue to indulge in such vulgar, self-pity."

"How dare you take me to task!" He censured, boring into her with his steely gaze which merely served to see his aunt thump her cane on the floor and continue in the same vein, abruptly standing up in anger. She pointed her cane in his direction and thrust it swiftly backwards and forwards as though to stab him with each word she uttered.

"I do dare, young man and will continue to berate you whilst you act in a manner so far beneath you." Pausing to take a breath, she continued,

"Your behaviour is scandalous to say the least and although I am loathe to give credence to gossipmongers it behoves me to state just how woefully you have indulged yourself in the dubious attentions of such as cannot be discussed in polite company."

"That is none of your concern, Madam," he snapped in abhorrence, acutely aware of his aunt's cronies who breathed gossip through every pore and were only too pleased to recount the minutest detail to this particular relative who was a renowned stickler towards duty, self-respect and family. Although he tried to silence her, he knew that she would not accept that he was a lost cause, even though his behaviour with his mistress, the delectable Sophie, and his drinking of late, were becoming somewhat of a problem.

He had not always felt this way. There was a time a few years ago, when he had loved life and enjoyed waking up every day. Now, it seemed a long time ago and all he had left was a feeling of emptiness and a sense of grievance. He was well aware that his aunt truly believed the once happy, carefree man was there buried deep inside him, but no amount of mistresses, alcohol or gambling ever raised a smile upon his face. Only his Aunt Constance could do that when she was not attempting to persuade him to do his duty.

He had the dubious distinction of being her favourite relative and knew that she genuinely cared for his wellbeing.

Meanwhile, she was not in the least perturbed by his high handedness and slowly raised a haughty eye designed to challenge the sting his words were meant to convey.

"You will cease this abominable behaviour forthwith." Her bony shoulders lifted and fell, then she heaved a long sigh and said,

"Being the man you are, I know you will do what is right, even if you have to sacrifice your own desires for a while."

A silence ensued as he digested her words. The only sound was the ornate clock on the wall ticking loudly adding to the tension in the masculine room. Sebastian strolled towards the fireplace and turned.

"What you consider to be right is not necessarily in my best interests or desires," he said in his cold, aloof manner. After releasing an impatient breath he continued. "I did not come to town to be harangued by you." Taking another healthy swig of his brandy, he moved closer to her and with a huge sigh he said in his forthright manner,

"Madam, I refuse to be manipulated in this way, by you or anyone else. I know what you are angling for and I am not desirous of conforming to your wishes. Moreover, I have no aspirations to re-enter the marital state merely to please my relatives, and you cannot expect me to replicate the same disaster that was Dulcie."

There, he thought, *I have said her name and for once there is no anger or shame or even embarrassment.*

"Good God no!" Lady Constance replied, stiffening her bony shoulders and breathing heavily as she tried to come to terms with what she felt was an insult. She resumed her seat and pondered for a while before changing the tone of her voice to a more congenial level.

"As to that, of course I do not wish for such a one as her to fill the role of Duchess. Heaven forbid, but only think Sebastian, you were sadly duped with the Ridley's, as were all of us."

She heaved a deep sigh, refusing to revisit the past even though she knew that it held secrets that needed to be uncovered.

"In addition," he stated ignoring her reply, "It is far too soon to be contemplating another relationship. The woman died nine months ago for God's sake."

"Oh no, Sebastian," she cried exasperated by his words. "She has been gone for well over twelve months, now. Don't you remember, it was the week before Christmastide that the accident occurred. You cannot wear mourning for ever!"

"Enough!" he yelled.

Quiet permeated the room as both thought of the debacle that ensued as the result of the arranged marriage between the then Lord Sebastian Winslow and

Lady Dulcie Ridley. Both their fathers had been close friends at Eton and it was their dearest wish that the families be united in marriage.

At that time, the two young people involved appeared to be fond of each other and as Lady Dulcie was the toast of London Society, and breathtakingly beautiful to boot, it was easy for the dashing, young, handsome Lord Winslow to fancy himself in love with her. Whether he fell so hard because he was still suffering from the loss of his twin brother, Andrew, he could not say.

The accident that killed him had happened nearly four years ago, just as Sebastian had returned to their country estate in Wiltshire. He had been at a house party in Somerset and soon after his return, his brother had gone out riding. Sebastian remembered refusing to accompany him as he was stiff and sorely in need of a bath after his journey.

His elder brother had fallen from his horse that day and broken his neck. Andrew, a bruising rider had misjudged a hedgerow although Sebastian knew he had jumped it many times before. He could only think that his brother's thoughts were elsewhere at the time. In any event, he hadn't stood a chance. His horse had fallen on top of him. From that day, he blamed himself for not accompanying him. If he had, perhaps they would have taken a different route. At least the doctor had said that his death was instantaneous which went a long way to easing the sorrow. Six months later, he had met Lady

Dulcie who dazzled him with her beauty and helped fill the emptiness he suffered during his grief.

Before their marriage, she had showered him with affection that went a long way to healing his sense of sadness and loss and he could not seem to have enough of her. Dulcie was the very willing partner to his intimate embraces and delighted in the love making stolen prior to their nuptials. Indeed, even after they were wed, for the first few months, they could not get enough of each other. The young Lord was besotted and would have done anything for his beautiful wife. Theirs, appeared to be a match made in heaven.

The day his parents died in a tragic carriage accident, was the day he inherited the dukedom which should have belonged to his brother. Sebastian never wanted the responsibility. It should have belonged to Andrew but it was not to be. Looking back, Dulcie became sullen after her first flush of pride in becoming a duchess as she wished to remain in town and be a prominent member of the ton.

When she realised that Sebastian expected her to share in his responsibilities and frequently travel to his vast estates with him, she became mulish. Even when they visited town, his mind was forever on the House of Lords which annoyed her further. She hated responsibility and was only happy when she could play hostess at balls and attend the many delights of the London Season.

Their feelings had cooled for each other rapidly during the first few months of inheriting the title and once she realised that she was expecting a child, the Duke's demand that she retire from her social life and return to Huxton Hall was the last straw. She obeyed him reluctantly, but their marriage was in name only afterwards and she did her utmost to make him and the servants as unhappy as she possibly could, often exhibiting tantrums, which he abhorred and throwing anything within reach when he ignored her.

Now, a widower for the last twelve months, his eyes were wide open and he had no wish to surrender his heart to anyone.

"Sebastian, my dear," her ladyship pleaded looking horrified. "Do not think anyone expects you to form a love match."

Indeed she truly believed it would take a miracle for one as emotionally paralysed as he to succumb to an ounce of feeling for another woman. Obviously, he had misunderstood and jumped to the wrong conclusion.

An ugly scowl marred his stunning good looks as he replied,

"Do you expect me to believe in love after what I endured at that she-devil's hands? Trust me, Aunt, I am not the greenhorn I was and I am not in the market for a wife who would expect my sole attention at every turn."

He sighed and appeared to shudder. He must make her understand him as he hated arguing with this woman.

"I am quite content with my situation at present and have no desire to change." He shifted uncomfortably, knowing that at least part of his words were lies.

God, I need a wife, or perhaps…. a brood mare would be more specific

Lady Constance shifted uncomfortably in her chair. She let out an unfeminine sigh, then recalled herself and straightened her spine surreptitiously.

"Of course not dear," she replied, attempting to regain any ground she may have lost. "And that is why I am here to propose an idea that could prove beneficial, whilst not inconveniencing you greatly. Please believe me when I say I do not expect you to make a love match."

Sebastian looked suspiciously towards his aunt not trusting her to begin to understand or resolve the burden he carried. At the moment, he could depend upon no-one to alleviate his current problem. He knew he had to beget an heir as soon as was humanly possible if he was to preserve the dukedom and protect his many dependants. As unpalatable as it seemed, he was conscious of his duty and if he failed to provide an heir, the alternative was unthinkable. That unthinkable was Lord Darcy Rutherford, the present heir. Once, not so long ago, this man was known as his very best friend. Now, he believed the fellow to be his worst enemy. This specimen of overly zealous, male pride had been a thorn in his side for the last year and stood to inherit all on his demise. Although he was his cousin, there was no love lost between them. Too much history separated them and would for an eternity and beyond. God forgive the hatred he felt towards him.

Although Sebastian held the dukedom, riches beyond belief and fruitful lands, it had been Lord Darcy Rutherford that had secretly appropriated the one thing that Sebastian had placed above all others. In the beginning of their tumultuous relationship Dulcie had been the air that he breathed, the one person in his life that he felt he had truly won instead of inheriting from his forefathers, but in this he had been sorely mistaken. Now he knew it had been his wealth and title that she had coveted, not him as a person and the hurt still pervaded his very being, rendering him paralysed and impervious to all the softer feelings a man might feel for the fairer sex.

After the death of Dulcie, Sebastian was sensitive to how peripheral life could be and to the uncomfortable feelings of vulnerability which surfaced whenever he thought of her, so he tried to reject them at every turn. Eventually, in suppressing those feelings, he believed himself immune to any woman that attempted to breach his armour.

Now it appeared that his aunt desired that he once again fall into parson's mousetrap and this aroused feelings of distaste that enveloped him and set his teeth on edge. Yet, deep down, he knew there was no alternative. He hated to acknowledge that his back was up against the wall and that his aunt was correct about his duty. Little did she know that it was a duty that was becoming more pressing by the day and that an heir was probably the most important link to preserve a heritage that was so important! He could not let his deceased father or brother down, let alone his numerous dependants.

His mind was in chaos as he admitted to himself just how imperative it was to beget an heir, but for the life of him, he felt he could never feel comfortable or trust another woman around him in his day to day life. Then again, what possible choice did he have? Just as the dense mist engulfed the sky, it served to emulate the feelings of loss. He often imagined himself floundering in a maze and not knowing how to find a way out to the freedom he so desired. A freedom from the strong emotions he had suppressed for so long and which he knew would never allow him to live a normal life ever again. God, he wished he'd never been such a callow youth

For the last few months, a number of accidents had occurred threatening his existence. Slowly, over time, he had reluctantly come to the realisation that his life was in jeopardy. The many mishaps he had experienced were not mere coincidence. Someone wanted him dead.

He had not shared this information with anyone except a hired agent that was presently trying to gather facts together. At the moment, the man had nothing tangible to disclose, but Sebastian knew that he would need to take positive action himself in the near future. The question he kept pondering in his mind was who he could trust to disclose what he knew to be fact and what was, in fact, conjecture or coincidence. People could be bought and he had lost close contact with many of his friends since the demise of Dulcie, burying himself in the countryside.

At present, the only person close to him was his aunt. Then again, she was want to gossip to her cronies so it was far safer for him to remain quiet. He had reluctantly come to believe that if his life was in danger and she discussed it with anyone, it could travel to the perpetrator and might place her in danger. It would be better for everyone if he kept the knowledge to himself. Moreover, he knew he could not lay this burden on her shoulders and besides, she could do nothing to help him.

Gradually, he became aware that his aunt was still speaking, while he had remained lost in his reverie. He slowly resumed his place in the present and tuned in to her words. His face softened. Bless her, she always thought of familial duty first and he knew how much she cared for him even though she exasperated him at times. She merely wished to see that he was happy.

"And she would not expect any untoward attention from you as she would quite recognise her place. Indeed, I do believe that you could stipulate the terms of the arrangement to suit yourself completely if that would be agreeable to you and without the discomfort of hysterics or nonsensical behaviour from her."

He stared at his aunt trying to understand her words.

What was she saying? Something about a woman!

His face softened even more as he looked at her. The fog slowly cleared and he became alert. Her old, familiar, beloved, countenance beamed at him as though she had offered him a prize beyond compare.

"I'm sorry Aunt Constance, what were you saying? I must confess I was in a brown study just then, wool gathering."

"I was explaining about my god daughter." she said, turning towards the tea tray and pouring herself another cup. She added cream and slowly stirred before continuing.

"Really Sebastian, it is too much. Kindly listen."

He tried to hide his smile at her scold. Such a small woman but such a big heart when it came to her family.

Her face softened and she continued with a gentle voice.

"About eighteen months ago, I had a letter from her mother who at the time was beside herself and extremely anxious. Like most parents, she was worried for the future of her daughter who had spent the last few years comforting her in her grief, which I might say was her duty after all. They lived in Somerset and I visited on many occasions."

The Duke patiently waited for her to continue, knowing that his aunt would take her time. He watched her closely as she paused to sip her tea. After replacing her cup, Lady Constance rose from her chair and straightened slowly, heaving a sigh as she did so. She walked across to the window and stared at the almost perfect scene in front of her. Well-tended gardens were before her yet it was not the scene before her eyes that occupied her thoughts.

"Dear Letitia and I spent so many happy times together in our youth." She paused, lost in her own dreams. A smile softened her face as she remembered some memory from the distant past. Another sigh escaped her while the Duke tried to assimilate her words. He watched her slowly turn towards him as though recollecting herself.

"My dear Sebastian," she implored. "Please listen carefully to what I have to say. Trust me," she almost pleaded, "I truly believe that this is extremely important to the future of the dukedom and our family as a whole."

Her demeanour was unusual as ordinarily, she said her piece without hesitation, but this time, she appeared cautious as though there was a certain nervousness which he knew was alien to her. He sensed her weighing his mood as she stared at him and then, he witnessed her instant decision to continue as though she was convinced it was the right way forward. Sebastian heaved a sigh but resigned himself to listen to whatever she had to say. Obviously, it was important to her. Sensing his capitulation, she returned to her seat and settling herself comfortably, she continued.

"Letty, my childhood friend, was widowed and became somewhat of a recluse. You may have heard of the Earl of Chingford, a rich and formidable person to be sure."

"I barely knew him," he answered, frowning to recall the man in question. "Old title I believe, yet I think he was one of my father's set in their salad days, but I don't believe they were life-long friends."

"They were to be sure. I believe he was in contact with your father before the accident that took my sister and him so tragically." A sadness played over her face as she thought of her beloved sibling. During the last few years, so many family members had perished. It had affected Sebastian more than he realised. She watched him closely as Sebastian walked towards the brandy on the mahogany side table and poured himself a generous measure. A look of disapproval stole over her face. She believed he was drinking far more than was good for him, but at the moment, she would not voice her thoughts. Far too much was at stake. As he turned to her she resumed her narrative.

"Anyhow," she continued, "he married Letitia the daughter of the Earl of Chester, some thirty odd years ago. For years, she hoped for a son, but it was not to be, much to his Lordship's displeasure." She sighed, then continued,

"Well, Arabella was born after three miscarriages and poor Letty has been unhappy for years because she so desperately wanted to provide him with an heir. She always believed she had let him down badly." She looked into the Duke's eyes, "She loved him, you know, even though he was never faithful to her. But that is by the by."

He heard an unladylike sniff and watched her shrug her shoulders knowing she would feel that it was not quite good ton to display such vulgar feelings. Turning away, he smiled to himself. His aunt was still such a romantic at heart.

"Anyhow, Letty's dying wish was that I assist Arabella in finding a husband and after spending the last three months with the gel, I feel she is the ideal person to fill the shoes of the future Duchess of Somerville."

Chapter Two

*A*stony silence pervaded the room as Sebastian glared at his aunt in absolute shock. He could not believe his ears. If he had heard correctly, she had just suggested that he should marry a complete stranger who would resolve the problem of his duty to his family. Furthermore, a lady, whom he had never met in his life, would provide him with an heir and ask nothing in return. It was unbelievable! In his experience, women did nothing unless there was something in it for themselves.

Indeed, only his strong sense of discipline coupled with decorum prevented him from laughing out aloud. But how was he to handle this? To begin with, he could not hurt his aunt however irritating she could be. He was well aware of losing his patience at the beginning of this interview, but she was thankfully unaware of the reason for it. If she had been privy to the conversation with his agent that he had endured prior to meeting her, she would have forgiven him his unruly outbursts.

"And what makes you believe that this paragon will suit me?" he asked, smiling softly in an attempt not to sound too patronizing.

"Well, as to that, you will need to take my word for it." she replied, beaming at him in a smug, satisfied way.

"My dear Sebastian," she continued as though she was the cat that licked the cream. "Although she is not beautiful in the normal sense of the word, she is accomplished in so many different ways and such a pleasure. Furthermore, she does not desire a love match. Indeed, she wishes to marry well for her mother's sake as she promised her that she would."

Looking slightly uncomfortable, she decided to reveal all.

"The other reason of course is that her father stipulated in his will that if she fails to marry before she is one and twenty, her vast dowry will be taken from her and she will be left penniless."

A bark of laughter escaped him.

"That is certainly an incentive for the young lady." Sebastian countered sarcastically, "but she may not wish to play second fiddle to a man whose first priority will always be the dukedom. You know that I owe it to my father."

"Yes, I know and that is why it is important that you give my notion serious thought," she replied. "Knowing her nature as I do, I am sure she will come to love the estates and responsibilities that go with them and she will probably positively bury herself in good works for the poor. After all, she has been involved with many charities for years."

Sebastian's face took on a cynical expression. "She sounds too good to be true."

His aunt stiffened, glaring at him in disapproval, becoming somewhat annoyed at his attitude.

"Arabella understands that she must do her duty by providing heirs and has been thoroughly trained as a hostess as well as with the workings of a large household. I swear there is no hint of coquetry in her manner."

"You are quite obviously her champion, my dear," he drawled in an attempt at levity. He took a swig of his brandy and settled himself in a chair opposite. "Sounds like a milk and water miss to me."

"On the contrary, she has much spirit when she is stirred to defend any one of her causes, but ordinarily, she is quite level headed and will not fly into the bows at a mere triviality. At twenty years, she does not dream of a raging romance and quite accepts the idea of an arranged marriage. Indeed, she told me only yesterday that she believes she considers herself on the shelf and will end her days as an old maid."

The Duke looked perplexed and frowned as he attempted to take in the context of her words.

"Does she realise the position she would hold as a future duchess?" he asked.

"Of course she would if she knew of my intentions for her," she replied, "but I have not mentioned your name in case you do not agree to my proposal."

The Duke looked at her and smiled. There was a decided twinkle in his eye as he said,

"You mean, my proposal, don't you think?"

His aunt let out a sigh much exasperated by him and replied,

"Please Sebastian, do not jest upon such a grave matter. Her heart may not be involved, but the child is a worthy wife for you and my earnest desire is that you two meet. She is of noble birth and if you think you would not be displeased with her, then we can forge ahead. No need to wait. She would not require a fuss so yours could be a quiet wedding."

"Aunt," he drawled, "Do you not think you are perhaps racing ahead a little?"

His smile was truly genuine as he continued. "You seem in an unconscionable rush to further my nuptials when I have not even had the pleasure of meeting the young lady in question yet."

"Indeed," she replied, looking a little embarrassed at her outpouring. "It is merely that I know she would make you a descent wife and would not wish to be the toast of London as did Dulcie."

A frown passed over her face as she thought of the woman who had inflicted so much damage. Then, replacing her torrid thoughts with another vision of her god daughter, Arabella, her face miraculously softened into a smile of delight. She looked up at him, and as though explaining to a child, she spoke slowly, saying,

"She is a gentle young woman, although perhaps not quite so young. As I said, she is twenty so is quite beyond the giddy stage of a debutante."

He gave a shudder. "Heaven forbid, I would not consider a debutante."

Much comforted that he would perhaps actually consider someone older, she continued,

"And Sebastian, I do not wish for you to hurt her in any way. Indeed, from all accounts, she has had her own share of heartaches."

"She has loved before?" He asked frowning.

"Of course not," she was quick to reply, "but there are many other forms of heartache that you would perhaps have not experienced."

"As you say." He drawled in what she thought was quite a provoking manner.

She sat up straight, once again twitching her skirts.

"I only wish that you could meet with her and see how you feel. She need not know that you are considering asking her for her hand, but if you like what you see, I would wish for you to offer for her as soon as you could as her mother passed away last year leaving her vulnerable to fortune hunters."

She smoothed an imaginary crease in her skirts and again seated herself more comfortably. He could tell she was nervously awaiting a response from him but he was unable to say anything at that particular moment.

"What is more to the point is that she turns one and twenty in two months, so for her, time is running out. My dear Arabella will have no protection from the evils of this world."

"Come Aunt," he returned, "that is doing it too brown when she has you as her champion, so needs no other to protect her."

"Alas, I will not always be here to protect her. I am an old woman. You may think she is safe, but there is one other in the framework that I cannot like and because of the immense fortune she is due to inherit, and given her attitude towards marriage and men in general, I am sorely afraid she will make the wrong choice."

"Not such a paragon then!" he drawled, dryly.

"No dear," she replied, "and please do not pull caps with me. She is merely an innocent, with a dowry of one hundred thousand pounds, who is presently being deceived by none other than your cousin, Lord Darcy Rutherford!"

****

Sebastian Winslow, the eighth Duke of Somerville, brushed a speck of imaginary dust off his dark blue superfine and checked his tight fitting, buff coloured pantaloons before he walked into Lady Constance's Green Room.

He was about to meet the Lady Arabella, the paragon that she had continually praised for the last seven days, while constantly calling on him and haranguing him unmercifully with pleas to at least meet the young woman in question.

To say he had his interest peaked would be truthful. More so, since his near miss with a runaway carriage late last evening! It would seem that the person responsible for his proposed demise would stop at nothing. This latest incident had forced his decision even though his dislike of the idea of marriage was still foremost in his mind. Thinking of sharing his life with a complete stranger was completely repulsive to him, but he knew in his heart that this visit might provide him with the solution he required. Perhaps she was the only answer to his present dilemma.

His father had made a marriage of convenience and over the years, both seemed happy enough with their choice, although he knew that he had looked elsewhere for many of his more intimate and erotic pleasures. He remembered his mother seemingly content with her life even though he knew she turned a blind eye to his father's amorous affairs. Such was the mode for many of the titled gentry, but Sebastian had never felt that it would suit him to follow in their footsteps.

He would have liked to have discovered the way out of his present quandary himself, but was beset by problems, and if he was truthful, could never have envisaged finding a respectable woman of good family whose aspirations were not motivated by a title or wealth.

Why did everything have to be given to him on a plate and worse still, why didn't he feel gratitude? How he wished he was the master of his own destiny, but as things stood, he could not afford the luxury of waiting for solutions by himself. His dukedom depended upon it. He only hoped that the woman was pleasant to the eye. It would certainly make bedding her a little easier.

Sebastian surveyed the occupants of the room coming to rest on his aunt. There were only two ladies present, the other, a tiny little woman, Lady Henrietta whom everyone called Hettie. He often referred to her as the jittery cousin, a woman of about forty years whose features would proclaim her relationship to the family anywhere. He remembered her as an irritation as she giggled nervously through conversations. His aunt appeared to be fond of her though which went a long way to his acceptance of her continual presence whenever he visited his relative. Fortunately, most of the time, she busied herself with her embroidery and very rarely participated. He remembered that she was quite a rich widow, but detested living on her own and preferred the company of his Aunt Constance. Family duty was important to Constance Peabody and she would invariably practice what she preached.

"Oh there you are, Sebastian." That lady warmly greeted him and pointed to a seat that looked to be most uncomfortable.

"You have just missed Arabella who is taking a turn in the garden." She turned to her companion, her face softening.

"Dear Hettie, could you go and fetch her for me?"

"Of course," Hettie answered, her eyes reminding him of an adoring spaniel. He watched her scurry away in search of the Lady Arabella.

Silence pervaded the room as a maid brought in the tea tray. It continued until tea was poured and they were once again, alone. She watched him fidget as though uncomfortable.

"I do not offer you brandy, Sebastian as I believe it is far too early in the day." She frequently lectured him about his drinking habits and he habitually ignored her on this point. Today though, was slightly different. A brandy would have helped as he was still slightly shaken about the near miss with a certain carriage and wondered what the next so called accident would be. He knew that if he related the circumstances to her, she would think differently, but he dare not tell her. He could not risk it.

His aunt looked stern as she passed him the insipid tea that he placed down on the table in front of him. He would not drink it. He hated the stuff.

"Thank you," he said, "remember, I am only here to look."

She gave him one of her piercing stares and said,

"I know, but I hope you will find her favourable as Rutherford was here again yesterday and when I told Waters not to admit him, he strolled in having the temerity to state that family did not stand on ceremony. His ways are too forward to be comfortable." She took a sip of her tea clearly annoyed by Rutherford's behaviour. Her next words clarified her feelings.

"To be sure, I cannot like his conduct. It is not seemly to be so encroaching and it is not as though he has close family ties with me." She shook her head from side to side and continued,

"He never used to be a visitor before Arabella came to us and I did not like his overbearing tone towards me when I tried to refuse him."

Sebastian frowned. "Good God, he has no claim on you. Yours is a slight connection. I will have a word with him and ensure he does not visit again."

She heaved a heavy sigh,

"I told him yesterday that Arabella was indisposed and I could tell by his expression that he did not believe me." She sighed, heavily, labouring her point to ensure that he knew just how incensed she felt, then made a point of expanding on her god daughter's mission of the day before.

"She was collecting books for me from the lending library with her maid to be sure, but I could not risk him rushing around to speak to her in public. It would not do for dear Arabella to be seen with such as he."

"It would not do for any single female. The man is a rake and a fortune hunter and I feel sure it is not Lady Arabella's attributes that interests him, but come," he countered, "knowing you as I do, you are more than capable of depressing the pretensions of those who fail to live up to your exacting standards."

"That being so, he is forever a thorn in my side and I am becoming too old to depress such as the likes of him."

"Nonsense, my dear, you have not lost your touch yet, even though you like everyone to believe you are in your dotage."

As he spoke the last words, the door opened and in walked a tall young lady with a gentle smile on her face.

"Hello Aunt," she greeted in a pleasant, melodic voice, "It was so lovely in the garden. Oh," she stopped in her tracks, "Hettie did not tell me we had company. She only said that you were desirous of my company in the Green Room. I'm sorry." She curtseyed and began to turn back towards the door.

"Come Arabella, we do not stand on ceremony. It is only my nephew, Sebastian, or if I am to use his formal title, his Grace the Duke of Somerville," and pointing to a seat opposite she said, "Sit down and have some tea."

After another curtsy, Lady Arabella greeted him with, "Your Grace," and slowly sat down and smiled at this most handsome of men. She quickly took in his overly long, shiny dark hair tied behind in a que then admired his piercing, blue eyes and lingered longingly on his perfectly shaped mouth. His bronzed skin spoke of a life lived mostly outside in the fresh air. Again, she was drawn to those thick, sensuous lips that at this moment she noticed were shaped into a smile.

She knew that he was her Adonis; the hero who had saved her from the wicked man some four years ago, having never forgotten his presence at the Charity Ball at home in Muchbury. Since that day, no-one else had ever measured up to him. Now, this close to him for the first time in years, she found it difficult to prevent her eyes from devouring his face.

I'm sure I could be forgiven for my feverish imaginations!

She took a slow calming breath as she continued to study him further. It did not seem possible that this man could improve with age but he obviously had except for perhaps a certain remoteness in his eyes. Now, he looked every inch a Duke in his bearing and air of command. She was truly intrigued by him. Slowly, she realised that she was staring and that his Grace was aware of it. She blushed and quickly lowered her eyes to the tips of her toes, embarrassed at her wanton behaviour.

But he is so handsome to look at, she thought.

Luckily, she was unaware that his Grace's lips had twitched at her discomfiture. Feeling a little sorry for the young lady sat in obvious discomfort, his Grace roused himself.

"Lady Arabella, do you like London?" He watched as her features grew pensive. "I hear that you are staying with my Aunt Constance indefinitely."

She looked shyly into his blue eyes.

"As much as I appreciate Lady Constance's generosity in asking me to stay with her for a few months, I must own to missing my home in the country, your Grace," she answered in her mellifluous voice which Sebastian thought he rather liked.

"And home is where?" he asked.

"A little town just outside Bridgwater." She replied, "Muchbury in the County of Somerset."

"I seem to remember visiting it many years ago," he mused." I have friends who live quite close to Muchbury. In fact, I believe we attended a Charity event one evening that was held to be quite successful. You may possibly know my friends, Lord and Lady Murray?"

"Indeed, your Grace, I do." she remarked, smiling, having regained her composure. "They were neighbours of ours and attend the Ball every year."

"And is it still as successful?" he asked.

"Oh Yes, your Grace. The Ball now takes place every year to help raise funds for the poor. Reverend Althrop has made the event very successful. That is to say until the recent death of his wife. She died of influenza. They had only married three years ago and he is lost without her. At present, he is assisting me in managing the local orphanage while we look for someone to take over the running of it."

The thought suddenly struck her that he would not concern himself with a country reverend or an orphanage and she suddenly became silent.

He had noticed how her brown eyes appeared to dance along to the melody as she spoke which culminated in a very pleasing result. This was obviously a point in her favour. He studied her as she poured tea for herself and re-filled his aunt's cup. At first glance, she was not noticeably beautiful. Her hair was a rich brown, braided around her head. Eyebrows made a perfect arch for her almond shaped eyes. A pert nose which gave her face an almost mischievous slant and a perfectly bow shaped mouth. No, hers was not a face of great beauty, yet he thought it was a pleasing face that came alive when she spoke.

Hers was not the blonde, blue eyed perfection of Dulcie, he mused.

On second thoughts though, his prerequisites for beauty had always been blondes with blue eyes and no other woman had ever held attraction for him in the past.

Even Sophie, his present mistress, lived up to his normal expectations of feminine beauty. Lady Arabella gave him pause for thought. He found himself imagining her dressed in more appropriate clothing for a duchess and perhaps a softer hairstyle.

After a brief scan of her figure he was unable to make a judgement as the plain, grey dress she wore did nothing to enhance her attributes, yet she held a certain attraction for him. The thought surprised him as this was only his first visit. Turning towards his aunt he noticed an actual smirk upon her face.

"Would you like to share what amuses you so, dear Aunt?" He asked in a condescending tone.

"Oh, nothing, Sebastian," she replied, smiling at him in a secretive way. "I was merely thinking how cosy this is having my favourite people with me."

Sebastian looked at his timepiece.

"I'm afraid I will have to break up this cosiness, my dear, as I really have a desk full of paperwork that beckons to me, but it has been a pleasure." Sebastian rose to leave.

"Arabella will walk you to the door or perhaps you have time for a brief stroll around the garden," she suggested.

Arabella rose and waited for him to say his goodbye to his aunt and then led the way into the hall. Closing the door, she walked a couple of steps and then stopped, turning towards the Duke. She really needed to speak to him on the matter that had troubled her since Lady Constance had spoken on the subject this morning prior to the Duke's visit. A conversation that afterwards had found her strolling through the garden in deep thought thinking through her dilemma.

With always a need to be honest, there were elements of embarrassment that she could not help but feel. It was difficult discussing what was in her heart with a complete stranger, more so with a handsome one.

"Your Grace," she began, "this morning, Lady Constance made me aware of her wishes that you and I should wed."

Good, I have made a start, she thought.

"She informed me that you may not wish for an arranged marriage, but that you believed it to be a duty to your family. I am sure, now that you have seen me, you must feel totally against it." She took a deep breath then continued, "I do understand, your Grace and you must not feel any mortification in speaking the truth to me. I assure you I will not be desolate as we are merely strangers who have met only once."

Although I wonder what it would be like to really be loved by a man like you, she thought as she almost drowned herself in the depths of his beautiful eyes.

He looked stunned at her honesty and wondered how he should answer. As he surveyed her earnest expression, he speculated what it would be like to indeed take the chance and marry this girl.

"I agreed with my aunt that we should meet, my Lady, so that we might discover if we should suit. I must confess I have not come to a decision on the matter as there are many factors we need to consider."

"I understand completely, your Grace," she replied, "It is merely that if you think we should not suit, I would quite understand," Arabella whispered anxiously. She felt embarrassed but knew that she was plain and that she would never be able to compete with his former wife. She took a deep breath "I do not think I could bare it if you formed a dislike of me because you were manoeuvred into a match you could not quite like."

He laughed. "Let me disabuse you of that misapprehension, my dear. That would never happen. No-one could force my hand at anything."

She glanced at him and beamed, her eyes shining like dark pools. "Yes, and that is how it should be, your Grace." She started to walk towards the door, "I hope you did not mind this conversation, but I felt we needed to be quite honest with each other."

He smiled down at her and her heart completed a double somersault.

"Yes, I do appreciate your honesty, my Lady," and as she continued to smile at him, he noticed dimples appear in her cheeks. No, she was not in his usual style. He studied her closely, taking in her expression.

"Tell me, what do you think of the balls and routs in London. Would you not miss them if you were to marry and live in the country all year round?"

"As I said earlier your Grace, I prefer the country."

"I hope you don't mind me becoming brutally honest. I cannot for the life of me understand a woman who would wed on a whim. Are you saying you would marry a total stranger, share his bed and have his children without love?"

She was shocked by his honesty and paused for thought. Would she? Not with just any man, she knew. With this man she would. How could she tell him that she was attracted to him in a way she did not understand? She knew she could not.

"Your Grace," she said, nervously, "I am sure you would find it difficult to understand how a woman could give up her freedom and as you say, live intimately with a complete stranger, but as you can see, I am not one of the blue eyed, blonde beauties of the ton who can take their pick of men. I have no claim to beauty and would be grateful for a comfortable home and a husband who would treat me with consideration."

He bowed, smiled and suddenly pausing thoughtfully, asked,

"Would you mind showing me the garden that you proclaimed to be so lovely? I think there are one or two pressing matters that we need to discuss."

Chapter Three

Sebastian strolled through the peaceful garden with Arabella and noticed how at ease he felt. He silently agreed with his aunt that hers was not a demanding presence. She had not spoken one word and seemed to concentrate on the beauty of her surroundings rather than demand his attention. He found her movements graceful and she was unaffected by the usual missish ways he deplored amongst females of the ton. Her manners showed a well-bred ease that spoke of her noble birth.

Yes, she would make an excellent hostess! No milk and water miss this one.

He could not help but compare her to his former wife who had demanded his attention continually and even his mistress who frequently draped herself over his person to gain his attention whenever they were together. Such feminine wiles annoyed him. Darker thoughts pervaded his mind as he realised he was becoming drawn into the air of innocence she exhibited through her gentle manner. An innocence he reminded himself that no woman was truly capable of.

Thoughts from the past jolted him into wondering if this young lady was playing a game and would inevitably show her true colours once she achieved what she desired. He had to discover if this was the truth so he stopped abruptly and turning, stared into her large almond eyes. Eyes that were somehow intriguing in their depths.

"It would appear you are required to marry to save your inheritance?" He asked, raising enquiring eyebrows.

She continued to stroll so he followed her. After a short pause she replied,

"That was one of the stipulations my father made in his will."

They walked a few steps both engulfed in their own private thoughts until Sebastian paused in mid stride.

"I do not know how much my aunt has told you, but I feel the same as you do in that we should be truthful with each other. I did not wish to marry again, yet the situation as it stands has forced my hand." He watched her face as a slight frown creased her face.

"Now, I find that I need to marry as soon as is possible. My only problem is that I have to find someone who will accept me under the terms that I offer. Tell me, Lady Arabella, would you be willing to marry me as soon as possible if you could accept those terms?"

Feeling a little shocked by his abrupt approach, she stated without preamble,

"I would, if it would be to your liking." She attempted to hide her complete shock at his forthright remarks, but felt the need to explain why she would accept a suit from him.

"You must realise that I am well past the normal age of making a good match and I am now merely looking for a pleasant companion who I could be on friendly terms with and perhaps have a family."

She looked down at the snowdrops, admiring their beauty. "You know of my circumstances and I quite honestly do not wish to become a burden to my godmother."

"And being past the normal age of forming a good match you are quite disposed to consider my suit?" he teased.

Smiling at his humour, she continued with her stroll through the gardens. He walked beside her as she was pushed to remark,

"Although, my aunt probably did not advise you of all the facts, I feel I must offer you a true picture of my present situation."

"If you wish," he said, frowning, wondering what she had been hiding.

So here it comes, he thought, *she has had liaisons with other men, but she will say that they meant nothing to her.*

"I was fortunate enough to be left a goodly sum and a home belonging to my aunt a couple of years ago. We were all shocked when she died suddenly, but she stated in her will that I was the only living relative she could stomach."

Arabella smiled fondly remembering the lady who had always spoken her mind but had a heart of gold.

"Suffice to say, I do not really need to marry for money, your Grace, although I am sure my godmother has advised you differently."

The thought shook him somewhat as he pondered on the reality of her independence and what it could mean to his plans if he decided in her favour. His aunt had obviously been playing matchmaker and would stoop to any lengths to see him married.

"As to that, my dear, she did say that you stood to lose your father's inheritance if you did not marry by the time you were one and twenty, which, forgive me I believe is in the imminent future."

"Yes indeed, your Grace, and she is correct upon that score, but I do not need my father's money and would rather it helped some worthwhile charity than see it go to someone unworthy, although a husband would probably think differently."

"The sentiment does you credit, my dear," he replied, feeling rather uncomfortable with his thoughts although still unable to believe she was as innocent as she portrayed.

Arabella smiled, continuing to walk on through the winding path where the promise of unfolding daffodils gently swayed in the breeze.

I'm afraid she has fixed upon the notion that I may fall for Lord Darcy Rutherford and is anxious to see me safely ensconced in the married state before he carries me away." She said, laughingly, thinking the idea preposterous. He has become a dear friend to me but we would definitely not suit." Arabella strolled on through the winding path. "I do not think he is yet ready to settle down. At the moment, I am the furthest person from his thoughts but my aunt will not believe it." She smiled shyly up at him inviting him to see how humorous the situation was. His face had assumed a stern demeanour so she continued wryly,

"My aspiration toward marriage is solely based upon my desire to have a family of my own and not because I must marry to preserve my inheritance. I would not consider someone such as Lord Rutherford if indeed he asked me, as I do not feel his desires lean towards a family of his own at the moment. At least, he does not give that impression although he has many interests I find rather surprising in such as he."

"I think you would be correct in that supposition," he replied a deep frown marring his good looks. "Forgive me, my dear but I agree with you that his aspirations do not include a wife and family and married bliss. You would waste away if you were to choose to attach yourself with the likes of a well-known rake. He would run through your dowry during the first six months of your marriage."

She narrowed her vivid eyes not truly believing that Lord Rutherford was indeed a rake and peeved that he should believe that he could not possibly be interested in her. He obviously alluded to her lack of beauty. She blushed, but continued,

"It has always been a longing of mine to have a large family, but I would settle for a small one if that was my husband's wish. Indeed, I really believe that now I am almost one and twenty, time is running out for me to fulfil those dreams."

He secretly appraised her, confused by her dowdy clothing when she was an heiress.

Why didn't she dress to impress especially knowing of my visit? Was it a trick she played?

Resolutely, he continued still a little confused by her.

"But do you not wish for a grand romance like other women?"

She continued to smile and looked away from him. How she wished she was as beautiful as the Lady Dulcie who had captured this man's heart. Not for her the grand passion, yet she would strive to make this man happy if he decided to go through with a marriage of convenience. It would not be difficult to feel a real affection for him as he appeared easy to talk to and she felt comfortable in his presence.

"I am well past the age of expecting romance. I merely wish for contentment and freedom to pursue my various charities." Deep down, she knew that she longed to be loved like other women but her father had drummed it into her for years that she was unlovable. She often thought that a fondness could grow between two people and she believed that if she was lucky enough to have children, she would strive to be a good mother. Perhaps her children would love her! That would indeed be compensation for the lack of a man's love.

Meanwhile, Sebastian was thinking on her words.

Various charities, indeed! The woman was professing to be an angel, but what choice do I have? I can always send her away to one of my estates in Cornwall if she proves to be false. Once she has given me my heir of course. ...No-one will make a fool of me again. History will not repeat itself. I am conversant with all womanly wiles.

His face was sombre as he turned to her after deciding to be honest.

Let's see how she feels when I lay down some rules.

"I feel I have to be blunt. My main reason for marriage is to beget heirs and I am far too busy to spend much time with a wife." *There, I have said it.* "It would be a marriage of convenience for me as I could not offer you my heart."

She looked pensive as he spoke the words and then appeared to consider him.

"I understand that completely, your Grace. A man with so many duties, would have no time to pander after a woman's needs and I for one would wish for the spare time to indulge myself in my hobbies, societies and charities as I have already pointed out to you." She walked on in silence for a while seemingly thinking and looking a trifle wistful.

"I would imagine many of my societies would have to be dispensed with as I would be taking on further, more pressing responsibilities as your wife. Perhaps, a fondness may grow between us if we were to share those responsibilities. I am sure when two people enjoy the same interests, fondness could grow. I would like that to happen in a marriage of convenience."

"Indeed!" he exclaimed.

"Please believe me when I tell you I would not look for love but would do my duty as a wife towards you. You would hopefully give me the children I so much desire and in return, I would be your hostess when required. I would not wish you to indulge me in any way. I am well used to being by myself."

My father saw to that! She thought, bitterly.

He studied her, thoughtfully, aware that he had not done her justice. On close inspection, her skin was smooth and flawless and he had a strong desire to touch and caress her peach like cheeks. Odd, he thought considering she was not in his usual style. Even more so as she did not send out any feminine wiles or lures in an attempt to seduce him. He paused in mid thought. His mind would not allow him to feel she was the innocent she portrayed.

"You honestly have no desire for romance?" He asked, not believing that a woman could be so self-possessed.

She laughed at his question. "None at all, your Grace. I have had plenty of years to form an attachment yet have not done so. Perhaps I am one of those ladies who do not experience the grand passion for someone. I am probably too down to earth in my ways to become highly romantic, so do not be anxious that you will raise false hopes in me."

They were quashed years ago!

The thought pleased him that there had been no others who had captured her heart if indeed he could believe her. It was a novelty that a woman of almost one and twenty could be so fastidious in her taste.

"Yes," he thought, "she could be the answer to my prayers. Unless of course, she was passionless!

The thought made him shudder as he would have to lie with this woman, a complete stranger to beget a child. Visions of trying to perform towards a cold blooded ice maiden filled him with horror and his thoughts reluctantly reverted back to Dulcie. He instantly pictured his former wife's selfish actions, her coldness towards those she felt beneath her; her passion for London and the various men she flaunted in front of his nose.

Was this woman capable of concocting scandals as Dulce had?

"Do you wish to stay always in London for the Season?" he pressed, knowing that he could not endure to accompany her on the endless round of entertainment. Furthermore, he had the Lords to consider and needed to participate in Government circles at odd times. He did not wish to replicate his former years, no matter how imperative it was to beget an heir. He disliked the hypocritical society that demanded the epitome of good manners and a strong moral code, while married couples participated in affairs and debauchery of mammoth proportions, living double lives. Until one was caught in a clandestine affair, society turned a blind eye. He would loathe the constant gossip, parties and balls one was expected to attend when in London. He would also loathe being cuckolded again and for the ton to feed upon his shame. Another vision appeared of those who had sniggered and laughed in his face.

"It is not my wish to become a great society hostess, your Grace. I would hate it although I would try to host parties when called to do so if my husband wished it of me. I did not take in Society because my looks are not in fashion. Perhaps if I had been blonde and blue eyed, my time would have been more exciting." She laughed to herself. "No, I can live without the giddy delight of the London Season I believe."

There was sincerity in her tone. This pleased him, but he had to establish from the outset that he would expect much of her, especially after his experiences with his former wife. He felt a little guilty about his bluntness, but needed to be explicit.

"I must state from the very beginning that I would expect full compliance in the more physical issues in marriage. I am a full blooded man so please forgive me for any embarrassment I might cause you. It is only our situation, such as it is, that qualifies a significant amount of honesty between us, even though it may offend your sensibilities." He cleared his throat and waited in case she might wish to respond to his words. She remained silent, patiently waiting for him to continue.

"In this I must ask forgiveness as it is not my intention to cause you distress. It is merely that I would expect you to comply fully with my needs in the bedroom and I mean fully! I would not envisage keeping a mistress if we should marry so would expect you to do your duty whenever I desired your company if you understand me."

She could not help the blush that invaded her cheeks but knew she had to be as blunt as he if all her dreams were to come true. The thought secretly pleased her that he felt he would not require a mistress. This she felt boded well for a couple beginning a life together. If she failed him, she would expect him to seek solace elsewhere, but at least she would have a chance to please him. Taking a few deep breaths to compose her unruly thoughts she ventured,

"I am sure your Grace that it is an important part of married life. I would always try to please you in this as I understand that a man has needs. If I did not please, after I had given you heirs, you would be free to go to another, if you understand me. I would not expect you to stay faithful to me. I merely wish for children." She felt she had said too much but tried to make him understand that she would not tie him to her. "Ours would be a marriage of convenience, after all."

For some reason, this did not please him. He felt a little piqued that she should not be attracted to him in a sexual way and that she would be quite happy for him to roam after she had given him heirs.

Was she really that cold? Would it be like making love to an ice-maiden?

He was known to be a good catch. Someone that many would wish to marry. So why, when he insisted to himself that he wanted someone who would not upset his normal routine, did he feel so indignant when this young lady appeared to be the very person who would not look to change his life in any way. He chided himself for feeling so contrary. As he glanced at her face, he thought he must put her coolness to the test as he couldn't and wouldn't marry someone frigid. He needed a woman with some measure of feeling or else any children would be faced with a cold mother.

As he moved closer to her, she felt his cool breath on her face. She was conscious of her heart beating rapidly and her breath becoming shallow.

He looked into her eyes and said, "On the other hand, there has to be some passion between us or else we could not produce a family together. I would insist upon this and would train you to please me, but at the same time, I would give you great pleasure."

Her stomach responded in somersaults at his words. Could her cheeks burn anymore? A thought struck her and her breath caught in her throat.

"But what if I displease you?"

He swiftly moved closer and she closed her eyes as he took her lips in a kiss that seemed to devour her. She was conscious that her body was responding in so many fascinating ways and she felt as though she was melting into him.

Her heart was beating rapidly as he deepened the kiss that seemed to stir her very soul. His hands roamed her body in a proprietary way that made her feel as though she was already his and she found herself with an overpowering urge to press closer to his masculinity as his tongue invaded her mouth. Part of her was frightened but another part felt exhilaration at his touch and she wanted so much more even though she did not know what to expect.

Her breathing became laboured and then without warning, he suddenly pulled away leaving her feeling bereft. *What must he think of me?* she thought as she tried to regain her composure. But then, breathing heavily himself, he replied,

"I do not think you will displease me. I will teach you all you need to know. Do you think you can accept my terms and become a willing partner in the bedroom?"

No cold fish, this one!

She did not understand his intensity. He aroused unbelievable feelings inside her; feelings she did not quite understand, but looking into his incredible eyes, she thought she could trust him.

"Yes." She replied sincerely, feeling so very sinful but more alive than she had ever felt before.

He looked at her peach like cheeks and then his eyes roamed her body. It took a while for his breathing to slow down to a normal pace.

"Then, do you think you could agree to a marriage of convenience? You must be truthful as I do not offer you anything more."

She did not need his love. She would have his children and be there for him when his heart was heavy and he missed his Dulcie. Her whole being went out to this man who had lost the love of his life. Somehow, and she did not know how, she would try to heal his hurt. Perhaps she would find a way. Taking a deep breath she tried for a lightness of spirit.

"I daresay I could."

Chapter Four

After the episode with Arabella, his now affianced wife, he was feeling a little shaken. They had returned to his aunt to advise her of the news and he had then taken his leave of them. His next stop was the Bishop to arrange a special licence as now he had made up his mind, he wished to be married as soon as possible. As he arranged the details he thought of his wife to be. Her response had shocked him. She might believe she was passionless, but her body told him otherwise. She had come alive for him and this boded well for the future.

Hers was not the only response that had shocked him, however. He would need to guard his heart from this woman. Had he merely added yet another danger to his life?

Once the arrangements were completed, he went to his club. He did not understand the intensity of his feelings. She was nothing like the blonde, blue, eyed Dulcie, yet she attracted him sexually. His would-be wife was far from passionless and he would do everything in his power to cultivate her response when she became his. That would be as far as their relationship would go. He promised himself that their association would be non-existent outside of the bedroom. After all, he needed a woman to have his children. He did not need her outside of the bedroom.

He would ensure that she knew her place from the start for his own sake. Not even Dulcie had stirred such animalistic feelings inside him. The thought terrified him! At the same time it excited him. He would enjoy teaching her how to please him. He had not felt this aroused for years.

On the shortest of acquaintance she had a way of looking at one that made one feel all powerful, male and virile. He felt as though he was going mad. He would have to visit Sophie although now, he was unsure whether she could arouse the feelings in him that a simple, innocent miss had managed to do.

He must remember at all times that she was a lady and not his mistress and yet his mind was wondering off into fantasies that only a mistress or a whore could fulfil. Why couldn't a wife fulfil the same desires as a mistress? He could not see a problem as long as he kept her buried in the countryside for his own pleasure. His mind was filled with fantasies as he drank his brandy and ordered a bottle.

"Sebastian," a familiar voice from the past roared. "It's been positively ages. How are you?"

No need to glance up to put a name to the face who had been one of his very best friends in his youth.

"Good to see you, James," he said. "How're Derry, Walt and Perry? I haven't seen them for years."

"I think they are all in town. Darcy as well. Saw him the other day. We'll have to celebrate the good old days."

Sebastian frowned not wanting to know too much about Darcy Rutherford, his heir presumptive. He still wondered if he was the person who wanted him dead. For expediency, he knew he needed to pretend all was well in that quarter.

"Let me know when. I'm at the Town House for the next few weeks and you can wish me happy. I am to be wed in two weeks' time."

"Goodness, Seb, anyone we know?"

"No, although you may remember her father. The Earl of Chingford."

"Yes, I remember him. Didn't know he had a daughter.

His daughter inherits. No heir as yet to be found but he left her well dowered."

"Good God, man, he was worth a fair penny; you cannot need the money. How did you find her?"

"I didn't. She's my aunt's god daughter."

"Well I think you should have spread the word and given us all a chance at her. I need the money more than you, God dammit. I'm at a standstill at the moment."

"Tell me a time when you weren't!" Sebastian laughed.

He thought of Lady Arabella and a frown replaced his laugh. As much as he liked his friends, he would hate to think of an innocent in the clutches of any one of them. That was if she was as innocent as she made out to be. Even if she was false, she certainly didn't deserve the likes of the fortune hunters who would squander her money on mistresses and gaming. As much as he was fond of his friends, he knew they were rakes and would never desire to settle down in the country with a family. He could offer her a home, a family and he knew instinctively, sexual satisfaction. Once again, his loins ached with the thought of her delectable body, or that much he had explored during the kiss they had shared. Two weeks seemed an age.

The two friends shook hands as Sebastian stood up and arranged a meeting for the following evening. He would spend some time with Sophie to assuage his passion and after that, he would focus all his thoughts on his wedding plans. He needed to buy Sophie a gift before he advised her that he would not be seeing her again. If it was expensive enough, his mistress would accept her conge without a scene.

****

A tall, faired haired man dressed in a long cape made his way to the rendezvous in Seven Dials. He looked surreptitiously around the dark, slum, turning his nose up at the filthy rotten garbage at every turn.

How did people live in these hovels?

He grew more impatient as the minutes ticked by. Jenkins was late and he grew more nervous with every minute. *I must get out of here and fast!* **He thought.**

Presently, he heard a sound and the dirty rogue appeared before him, smelling of the garbage that lay all around. He turned his fastidious nose up and barked,

"You idiot! How did you fail again? The man must have nine lives for God's sake."

"I knows," Jenkins replied, wiping his nose on an already filthy sleeve, "but he's a fly one he is! Dived out of the way before we could run him down, he did."

"Next time, do not bungle it," the gentleman warned, "time is of the essence."

"I knows, Sir, but he be the hardest man to kill."

"Next time you will succeed!" He stated. "We will meet tomorrow evening in the usual place and do not be late!" Jenkins gave a swift nod and disappeared into the swirling mist.

Without further ado, the gentleman moved speedily out of the slum and vanished into the darkness. He would need to bathe to get rid of the smell of the Dials. Later, he would go to his club.

****

The next day, Sebastian was busy looking through an assortment of papers to be signed and invitations to various balls, routs and parties. With his usual aplomb he threw them in the bin.

Why do they bother to invite me when they know I will not attend? He paused to sip his brandy.

Returning to the papers, he examined a report on his estate in Wiltshire. Beddows, the steward, was doing an admirable job in his absence. How he longed to be there instead of in London. Duty called to him, though! He had to attend the House tomorrow as a motion needed his vote. After this week, he would be free to go down to the Hall to ensure everything was ready for his wife to be. He would not be taking her to Wiltshire just yet as he needed to be close to London for the sessions. Later, he would retire there, where he knew he could relax and enjoy his life.

A knock aroused him from his musings and the elderly butler, Danvers, who had served the family for many years, walked in to announce the arrival of Lord Rutherford.

He liked Danvers and he was the only member of his large staff except for his valet, that travelled with him from property to property. Danvers knew his ways better than anyone.

"I took the liberty of saying that you were busy, your Grace but he said he would not keep you above five minutes."

Annoyed at the interruption and at the unwanted visitor, Sebastian thought for a while if he really needed to see the gentleman in question. A small part of him wondered what he wanted. If indeed he was the person attempting to kill him, at least he would be safe in his own home where his servants were present.

Better to see what he wants!

He asked Danvers to show him in.

"Very good, your Grace," and the butler bowed himself out of the study. He was heard walking slowly over the marble floor of the entrance hall until he paused and beckoned Lord Rutherford to follow.

The tall, fair haired gentleman in question strolled into his Grace's study and sank himself into the leather chair opposite Sebastian's desk as though he had every right to be there. There was something of a challenge in his eyes as he made himself comfortable, crossing his legs and clasping his fingers together in a relaxed manner as though he had all the time in the world rather than a mere five minutes to state his business.

"Hello Cuz," he beamed, "I hear your tying the knot again," he drawled, in a deep voice, the smile never leaving his face. "I have come to wish you happy."

Sebastian looked at him with disapproval written all over his face. He was both irritated and somewhat affronted by his cousin's nonchalant attitude as though there was no history between them. Darcy was a rake but even Sebastian had to admit, he didn't look like a killer. His relaxed manner, the continual twinkle in his eyes and his love of women and cards proclaimed him a rake of the first order. Sebastian had to admit, the man always smiled. Perhaps that was a part of the charm that the ladies undoubtedly fell for. Doubts assailed Sebastian. In his opinion, murderers didn't smile. Then again, best friends as they were a couple of years ago, didn't cheat with their friend's wife. No, he did not trust this man before him.

"Since when have I needed or in fact wanted your good wishes?" he asked, coldly.

"Now, now, Cuz. You still have the wrong end of the stick, you know. I never did do what you accused me of. You will realise it one day. Truth will always out as it were."

Sebastian hands closed into fists and breathing deeply he pounded them loudly on the desk saying,

"You were seen. A tall fair haired man who resembled me, they said," and leaning forward to emphasize his words he accused, "You were seen with her just before she died."

Any other gentleman would have at least flinched at his Grace's tone, but not Lord Darcy. He continued to smile, lazily at Sebastian and heaving a sigh said,

"A tall, fair haired man may have been with her but I swear to you it wasn't me." Darcy's face grew more serious and earnest.

"It could have been anyone, but you decided it had to be me." He sighed, deeply. "In your supposition, you were wrong, dear chap. As I have repeatedly told you, I was with someone else at the time. I would not allow that person to vouch for me then, and I will not ask her now. Neither will I tell you now. One day perhaps, if she changes her mind and accepts my suit…………… That's if I live that long!"

"What the devil are you talking about? Sebastian asked.

"Are you trying to tell me you have proposed to someone and kindly expand on that last statement?"

"Hmm! I am interested in someone, quite seriously as it happens, but she won't have me."

"Wise woman! An heiress, I suppose."

"No, actually. She has a small independence but nothing to speak of. Besides, I do not need money. I have plenty of my own. For the last couple of years I have been making sound investments and they have paid off considerably."

Sebastian lifted his eyebrows in surprise. "That is not what the gossips say. They speak of your gambling and womanising. Kindly spare me your lies."

Darcy laughed. "You take too much notice of the gossips, Sebastian. They believe what they want to believe. I do not care what they say and often I encourage them so that they don't throw their daughters at me. I have gained a considerable sum from my investments in shipping but I don't advertise the fact to anyone. Sometimes, one needs to keep their cards close to their chest, Cuz."

"You are still not telling me what you meant by the second part of your statement. May I remind you, 'if I live that long,' if I heard you correct. Are you ill?"

"No, Cuz. I thought you might like to throw some light on why I have been attacked twice in a matter of a week. Both times as I left my club. I wondered if I might lay the blame at your door!" Darcy said as he studied his impeccable nails. "Strange how it happened when you came to town."

Sebastian was astounded by the devil's effrontery.

"You are joking, of course. Why would I bother myself with the likes of you?"

"Well, cuz, you have hated me with a passion since you took it into your head that I was having an affair with your wife. I still deny it, mind you, but you're the only one I know who has the motive to want me dead." He stood up and walked to the mantelpiece and examined a small figurine, picking it up with care as he was well aware that it was worth a fortune, then continued.

"These men meant business. It was only because a couple of strangers were in conversation close by and came to my aid, that we are able to have this meeting today."

"You said there were two separate occasions."

"The second night, I had Biggs and Saunders, wait close by in case I had need of them, which I did. Fortunately for me, they saved my life. I was lucky because one of them had a knife, but Saunders is quite a handy fellow to have around and I owe him my life."

Sebastian, leaned back on his chair deep in thought. Could he believe him? He knew who the men were who came to his assistance the first time. They were men he hired to follow every move Darcy made. He had arranged it so to try to save his own life. If he was telling the truth, something crazy was going on and he needed to get to the bottom of it at once. If Darcy was innocent of attempting his murder, then who else could possibly want him dead? He didn't know but by God, he would find out.

Best keep the tail on Darcy a while longer just to make sure he is innocent and perhaps to protect him as well. If I am wrong about him, I could be wrong about who had been with Dulcie the day she died.

"Contrary to what you may believe, I do not want you dead. I do want an heir, however, as I do not believe you would become a good duke should anything happen to me."

Darcy laughed, "Is that why you are marrying Lady Arabella, Cuz?" He strolled back to the chair and settled himself comfortably placing one leg over the other.

"I agree, I would make a hopeless mess of the dukedom. Not cut out for all that. I wish you luck and hope you have many sons. Believe me. I don't hanker after becoming duke. I have bought a fine estate close to your own in Wiltshire actually, and have discovered a fondness for renovating and developing it. Never did like the old abbey my father left me. The new estate needs some renovation and ironically, I discovered that your Lady Arabella has an interesting mind. She has many novel ideas about estate management. I found her conversation quite inspiring as it happens."

Sebastian was quite annoyed that Darcy appeared to know more about his future wife than he did. "Why were you visiting Lady Arabella?" he asked.

He shrugged his shoulders then appeared to look in the distance, deep in thought.

"I thought we might suit, truth to tell, but I was wrong. I didn't want a love match, just someone to settle down with; someone who could help me forget. But as much as I admire her, Lady Arabella is not for me. She deserves someone better. I have it bad, you see. Every time I thought about settling down, another lady's eyes would remind me that there is someone special who I need to win and I now know I must wait and hope. No-one else will do for me, Cuz."

He sounded quite genuine, but his faith had been badly shaken by his first wife's numerous affairs and Sebastian felt he could trust no-one at the moment. Still, it was better to keep Darcy close so that he knew what he was up to.

"I will have my secretary send you an invite to the wedding. That will put a stop to the gossipmongers," he said, wondering if he was going quite mad. There would be plenty security men present so he did not feel too concerned and he would have someone watch him closely.

"Thanks, Cuz. I will be please to attend, but you will never put a stop to the gossipmongers." With that, he stood up and took his leave.

"Darcy," Sebastian called, "Take care."

"Don't worry, I have something important to live for, Cuz," he replied and disappeared into the hall.

Sebastian heard the front door close. Silence permeated the room except for the clock ticking relentlessly on the wall. He sighed as his thoughts tried to conform into some kind of order. For so long he had believed his cousin to be a reprobate; one of the most dissolute rakes in London, but now he wondered if he had been duped like the rest of society. Did he really listen to gossip rather than base his judgement on his own instinct? To be sure, prior to Dulcie's death, Darcy would have been the last person he would have envisaged having an affair with his wife. When they were young men, he had been a part of his friendship group and often they had shared pranks with his brother, Andrew. His eyes softened at thoughts of his sibling.

The fateful day when Dulcie died at the house party, had changed all that and Sebastian had hated Darcy ever since. Oh, he had professed his innocence but the gossips had mentioned an affair and somehow it all seemed so plausible. Sebastian had felt a deep sense of betrayal. Not by his wife. She had flaunted her lovers often enough and he had ceased to care about her. It was Darcy who he felt had betrayed him. Now, if Darcy was telling the truth, he was guilty of a huge injustice towards his heir. At the moment, he didn't know what to believe."

The cards had been stacked against him from the outset. There were at least three people who said that they had witnessed a fair haired gentleman talking to Dulcie. The gentleman was seen embracing her before the accident that had taken her life. Moreover, they believed it to be Lord Darcy Rutherford. No other man present at the house party was tall and fair.

Sebastian had, at the time, become cynical, because of the many men his wife paraded before the ton. She had made him a laughing stock. The last few months, when he had insisted she live in the country, she had disobeyed him and spent most of her time between the townhouse and Huxton Hall, and while in the latter, had arranged huge house parties where the ton flocked in their select numbers to enjoy dubious entertainments that Sebastian felt beneath him.

His wife, while pregnant with what he hoped had been his child, flaunted lovers before him and held the most profligate parties belittling his name. No matter what he said in an attempt to put a stop to her behaviour, she had ignored him and laughed in his face. She had been out of his control, shaming the dukedom. No other woman would ever get the chance to do that to him again. He would be the one in control and ensure that the next woman he married would obey him in all things.

****

Arabella scrutinized the mirror examining her reflection. So she was to be married. Her very own Adonis!

He had been the reason that she had refused all offers for her hand. Each time she refused someone, her parents had rung their hands in frustration. In the end, her father had placed a stipulation in his will that she must get married by the time she was twenty one.

He had come like a Prince to save her from a celibate life. She would be forever grateful for that because, after seeing him, and experiencing his lips and hands on her body, she knew that no other person could ever possess her. Like a love sick child, she had waited years for someone who would replace him in her dreams. After a while, she had given up all thoughts of men and had concentrated upon her various charities, set up in Muchbury.

As she had said to the duke, financially, she was wealthy and had no requirement to marry, but she longed for a family of her own. She knew she didn't love the duke. It was merely physical attraction. She remembered back to what should have been her first season. It had been postponed because her aunt had died. Then, the next year, her father had taken ill and her mother decided to postpone her season for another year. He had lingered bedridden with his temper frayed because he was unable to go to London to his mistress and had taken it out on Arabella and her mother. When he informed her that he had changed his will to ensure she married before she was twenty one, her mother had agreed wholeheartedly with him.

Surprisingly, his health improved and when he felt well enough to travel, Arabella was fitted out with new clothes for her season. Unfortunately, her mother's taste in clothes with the new fussy flounces and deep swags and festoons, did not suit Arabella's tall, slim frame. She felt awkward and believed that her time in London was a complete failure. She had received numerous offers admittedly but they had mostly come from lonely widowers or fortune hunters. No-one stirred her emotionally, at least not enough to contemplate marriage.

She had heard about Lord Winslow's marriage to the beautiful Dulcie and she had watched from afar and followed their careers as leaders of the ton until they had retired to the country and then she had not heard anything more until the news of Dulcie's tragic accident.

Then her own father had died suddenly. Arabella and her mother retired to the country and a little over two months later, her mother became seriously ill. The next few months were hard ones as Arabella nursed her. Eventually, she died as well, leaving Arabella to the kind ministrations of her godmother, Lady Peabody. She had left her charities in the hands of Reverend Althrop who sent her progress reports, periodically.

It was a shock to discover that the duke was the nephew of her godmother and an even greater shock to hear of her plans for them both. Now she could hardly believe that she was to marry him. She knew that she could never expect anything remotely like love but at least she could have the benefit of his presence every day and every evening, even though the thought of his closeness and sharing his bed made her blush. She would do her duty though, knowing that he would want heirs. Yes, she anticipated doing her duty. Her body positively tingled at the thought of it.

Meanwhile, her days would be filled with fittings and the like to make her presentable as his duchess. She would not cringe at the cost because she would be able to do so much more for those in need once she was wed. He would not wish her to be forever clinging to him once they were married, so she would still find time to help those who needed a helping hand. So many people lived in poverty and the answer was certainly not as she had envisaged as a young woman.

People did not need to be given money as much as they needed training and the potential to dream of a better life and that better life made possible for them. They needed goals to reach and assisting them to reach their goals was so much more important than physically passing them money to squander in the public houses. That was not the way.

Endow them with a sense of self-worth and the tools to forge a future. Yes. That was the way forward. She had so much to do. She would probably see her husband a couple of times a week, if she was lucky.

Her godmother had been a positive treasure when she realised that she was to be married to the duke.

"My dear, I am so glad we did not buy you a wardrobe before Sebastian met you. To be sure, he would not have countenanced a match between you if he had realised how beautiful you are."

Arabella laughed looking fondly at her godmother who insisted that she call her aunt. "Nonsense Aunt Constance, you are being ridiculous! I am not a beauty so do not fill my head with thoughts that can only arouse false hopes in me."

"Don't be silly, my love," her Ladyship replied, "We are to go to Madame Therese tomorrow and she will fit you out in the most alluring wardrobe. You will be the toast of the town."

"But Aunt, his Grace does not wish to do the London Season"

"I know , but there will come a time when he will wish to show you off to all society and you will then take the ton by storm, my dear. Please believe me in this."

"If you say so Aunt, but I cannot see that day ever arriving and I have not taken in society as you well know. Neither do I have any interest in it."

"You will, eventually, my love."

"But I have had very few invitations since coming to live with you and only one gentleman caller whom I could not consider was really interested in me as a person."

"That, my dear, is because, since you have been with me, I have purposely played down your exceptionally good looks. Trust me, my love, the ugly duckling is now to become a swan."

Madame Therese was all that Lady Peabody had described. At first, she appeared disinterested, but upon hearing that Arabella was to become the future Duchess of Somerville, her attitude changed. Measurements were taken and advice given to Lady Peabody about hairstyles. Arabella's dark hair, when released from the tight confines of her braids, waved thickly around her face and down to her trim waist. Madame Therese believed a simple, softer style with elegance, would enhance the lady's unusual assets.

"To be sure, you need to make her eyes more prominent and her hair, just so. If you do as I say, my lady will be the belle of any ball. She will become the toast of London if you will follow my lead and keep her style simple and sleek."

Many gowns were ordered and promised for the following week. Arabella loved the materials in rich greens and blues. Even a burnt orange was selected in a rich silk material that she felt would feel wonderful on her skin. Bonnets, gloves and slippers were next on the list and by the time the two ladies arrived home, they were exhausted but very satisfied with their purchases.

In the days that followed, there were more shopping trips and eventually, worn out, she was ready and prepared for her life as the future Duchess of Somerville.

Chapter Five

*H*is Grace decided that they would travel to the country and be married in the small chapel on one of his closest estates to London. It was where Dulcie had spent most of her time when not in the capital. He would travel on ahead a week before hand to prepare everything.

Sebastian hated Huxton Hall where they would marry, but he felt in a way it would be a reminder not to get carried away by his bride to be.

After paying off Sophie, much to that lady's anger, he was without a mistress, so now he would indulge himself fully in his wife. She appeared virginal, but God help her if she proved to be false. If so, he would do everything in his power to get her with child and then find another bit of frailty to fulfil his needs. He reminded himself that he would not succumb to his wife's womanly wiles.

Huxton Hall was a stark, sixteenth century building that did not lend itself to any comfort. Its convenience was merely its proximity to London. He had invited his aunt, her companion and a few of his friends to the ceremony and afterwards to a small dinner party

Once married, he could concentrate on begetting an heir. The quicker it was done, the speedier he could resume his life and discover who was out to kill him.

****

It was cold but sunny, the day that they travelled down in the carriage. Hetty was beside herself full of excitement about the forthcoming wedding and twittering away to Lady Peabody about the happy couple, while Arabella sat quietly in the corner listening with a perpetual smile upon her face.

Hetty was repeatedly heard to say the words, "But it is so very exciting," and giggling and glancing dreamily at the bride to be as though she was a real live princess.

As the coach moved steadily along, the gentle sway of the carriage lulled Lady Peabody and Arabella into sleep and silence reigned until Hetty glanced out of the window to see a lone horseman travelling past them on a magnificent white horse.

"It is not for me to frighten anyone and indeed, I would not wish to do so, but you hear of dangerous highwayman and murderers on the roads these days. I cannot like to see a horseman travelling at such reckless speed," she said to no-one in particular.

Lady Peabody stirred and peered at her companion through eyes still hazy with sleep. By the time she was fully awake, she showed signs of losing patience with Hetty and as her cousin read those signs all too clearly, she elected to remain silent for a while unless spoken to.

Arabella gave an unladylike stretch and yawned. "Well if he is a highwayman, Hetty, he is no threat to us. He is riding far away from us, not towards us. He would be a very brave man indeed to hold up our coach when there are at least eight outriders and two coachmen to protect us." She was surprised by the duke's insistence that they travel, accompanied by so many.

"Yes, but he could be going to advise his associates that there is a large entourage driving on this road. Mind, I am not one to attempt to frighten anyone. Only, it did seem strange that he should be racing in such a fashion."

"Pray, do not fret so," Arabella replied softly, "We are quite safe."

"Oh, I know we are. How silly I am! I was merely musing on what might happen but I would not like to distress anyone."

"I swear I will be sending her away if she continues to fatigue me so." Lady Peabody moaned when they stopped for refreshments.

"Oh aunt, she means well." Arabella offered, trying to hide the smile threatening to spread over her face.

Luckily, nothing untoward happened on their travels and they arrived safely at the old Hall to be met by the butler and housekeeper who stressed that his Grace was busy with his agent. The dour looking housekeeper asked them if they would be like to be shown to the rooms allocated to them.

Arabella was given a beautiful suite where Molly was already in residence, unpacking.

"Oh, my lady, I will soon have your gown prepared for the wedding. Is this not a beautiful suite of rooms?" Arabella surveyed the room which was decorated in cream and gold.

"Yes it is, Molly and thank you. I will need you to prepare me a bath."

"I have already taken the liberty of ordering one for you, my lady, so please relax while I finish off here," and with that, she continued unpacking while Arabella and her aunt were offered refreshments. Arabella was becoming nervous now and would be glad when the ceremony was over. She hoped all would go well but discussed her fears with her aunt.

"My dear, all brides are nervous but you have no need to be. Sebastian will be a good husband. You must trust me in this. There is no other man that I would feel would suit as much as my nephew. He will be good to you."

"I know he will. It is just that we do not really know each other and things may be difficult between us. What if he forms a dislike of me?"

Lady Peabody laughed. "My dear, I am sure he will not do so. It is only nerves that are causing your distress."

"To be sure!" Arabella smiled. She vowed not to let her nerves ruin a perfect day.

Meanwhile, Sebastian was in his study receiving an update from the agent he had hired to watch Lord Rutherford.

A short, portly gentleman, he was rated to be very good at ferreting out information.

"My sources tell me that Lord Rutherford was dining in his club with his friends when you had the narrow escape with the runaway carriage, and there are many that can vouch for him, your Grace."

"Damnation, I would have bet a florin to get a crown that he was involved in some way. After all, who else would profit from my death?"

"Since then, I have followed him in case he had an accomplice and have also had his house watched day and night. Please believe me, your Grace, he has not put a foot wrong and does nothing to make me suspicious of him."

"Did I not leave instructions for more men to be put on the case? What further calamity must beset me before I find the culprit?"

"Your Grace, Lord Rutherford sustained two heavy beatings outside his club on two consecutive nights. As I told you last week, our men saved him the first time and we think it was his own men on the second."

"Yes, he did tell me about the beatings and whoever was responsible seemed to seek his demise. Can it be that the same person is seeking to kill both of us and if so, who would want us both dead and for what reason?"

"I do not know, your Grace, but it seems too much of a coincidence that both of you are under grave threat at the moment."

A silence ensued while the men were lost in their own thoughts.

"I would certainly like men to continue to follow my heir for the time being and I think we need to be posting more men around the estate."

"Please believe me, your Grace, I have carried out your instructions to the letter and have at least forty men posted here at present. No one can move without one of us knowing what they do."

"I certainly hope so, Colby, because there is much at stake. Leave me now and go check on your men."

Colby bowed himself out of his Grace's presence.

The meeting with his agent had brought disturbing memories to the fore. The last five years had seen many tragedies in his family. Dulcie had died with her unborn baby, having slipped down the stairs in this very house. No-one had seen her fall to her death and he had presumed that she had felt dizzy, hence the fall. Now his thoughts turned a little more macabre. Could she have been pushed? It seemed a fantastical notion but there was certainly a possibility that she had been murdered.

The attacks on Darcy changed everything and his mind was reeling with thoughts that he would once have dismissed as preposterous. Now, he wasn't so sure. His parents had died in a carriage accident but no-one could explain how and why they had taken the cliff path on that fateful night. At the time, they were returning from one of their estates in Cornwall which they had visited frequently. His mother had loved the estate and the surrounding countryside. Could someone have caused the accident that saw the coach hurtle over the cliff and kill his parents and the two coachmen?

His brother had fallen from his horse. Andrew had been a very experienced rider and Sebastian could never understand how he misjudged a fence that he had jumped many times. Dear God, had someone killed his twin as well?

Was there a jinx on the name of Winslow or did someone wish to wipe out the whole family? If so, and it was a daunting thought, who and why?

Another unwanted thought came to him. If these terrible suspicions were indeed true, would his new wife's life be in danger as well? He would need to have a guard in place for her just in case the maniac, because the person could be nothing else, decided to strike again. He shook his head to try to eliminate the unwanted thoughts swirling around his head. He was being ridiculous and needed to regain his common sense. Of course the deaths had been sad accidents and he needed to pull himself together.

Peace infiltrated his study, but he knew that beyond the door all the staff were putting the last preparations in place for the wedding. He took the time to think a little of the future with his new wife. She would run this household while they resided here and that should keep her busy and out of mischief.

The house was large, so they would not have to be always in each other's company. For her safety, he would ensure that she was never alone. He had enough staff to keep her safe.

His thoughts had shook him to the core. He would need to discover who would inherit if something happened to his heir and probably even further down the line, just in case his unwanted theories were correct. His solicitor would provide him with all the information he required. At least he was doing something about the problem now. For the first time in months, he felt more in control. There seemed to be a pattern merging and he hoped he was at last on the right track.

****

She was truly beautiful in a way that he had never envisaged.

The gasps from his family and friends had given him a jolt of discomfort and he squirmed filled with resentment at the knowledge that he faced a marriage to a raving beauty once again. It was strange how he had not seen further than his nose.

Arabella's hair was arranged in a simple wavy style tied up in a loose knot that softened her face. She wore a pale peach dress that highlighted her glorious skin to perfection. This was the first time that he had seen her in any other colour than grey. Somehow, she was transformed from a dowdy, ordinary young woman to this young beauty, who could hold her own in any company.

The dress she wore clung to her voluptuous curves as she glided towards him, her eyes shining like stars and her smile showing dimples that were there to be kissed and caressed. He was carnally conscious of her throughout the ceremony and his body throbbed in anticipation of knowing this woman who stood beside him, a look of complete serenity on her face. The thought annoyed him that she did not appear as moved by his presence as he was by hers. Why didn't she suffer the same pangs that he did?

He was glad when the ceremony was over. How he hated having to endure the congratulations of everyone present. His mind was questioning every one of them as he shook their hands.

Almost any one of the people present could be the person wishing to kill me and at this moment I am entertaining them.

Furthermore, his wife was spending more time with his friends thoroughly enjoying their congratulations which irked him.

What else were they whispering in her ear?

The thought angered him that they were delighting in her attention when it should be him, taking her to his room and making her his. Frustration mounted within him. He must rid himself of his guests as soon as possible.

It was not a love match! There was no need for all the platitudes. It was merely a business arrangement.

Meanwhile, he was trapped by his aunt and her cousin apprising him of the latest gossip around town.

As if I wish to know! At the moment, there is only one thing I am interested in!

Throughout the wedding feast, his aunt continued to monopolise his attention, but he was aware of his closest friends teasing and drawing laughter from his wife. She had never laughed with him as she did at this moment, annoying him further.

He was conscious of their opulent praise of her beauty which incensed him as he pretended to listen to yet another story from his aunt. Afterwards, they all returned to the drawing room to partake of tea. Once again, his friends monopolised his wife and he was forced to keep his aunt and her companion amused.

The only person that stood to one side, seemingly deep in thought was Lord Rutherford.

Should I tell him of my suspicions? He would probably laugh them off and accuse me of insanity.

The thought of something happening to him, because he had failed to warn him, made him feel uncomfortable. Perhaps he owed it to him to at least put him on his guard. Sebastian excused himself from his aunt and strolled over to Darcy who was staring through the window at the lawn that sloped down to a vast lake. He turned slightly, smiling ruefully and greeted him on his approach.

"You are most fortunate, Cuz," he said, patting him on the shoulders. "I wish you all happiness with your new wife. You see me all jealousy. If only I could bring a certain young lady around to my way of thinking. Then you would be wishing me happy as well."

"Patience, Darcy." Sebastian stated, frowning at his heir's words. He was shocked as he glimpsed a sadness in his eyes that he had never seen before. For as long as he had known him, Darcy was always laughing either with him or at him.

"I need to speak with you for a moment. Meet me in my study in five minutes." With that, Sebastian returned to his aunt, leaving Darcy with a slight frown, confused and slightly surprised, as this was the first time that Sebastian had accorded him anything other than polite tolerance in a long time.

Once the two men faced each other in the study, Sebastian did not wait to come straight to the point.

"Has anything else untoward happened to you since we last met?" He asked, watching his reaction closely.

A look of utter surprise passed over his face, before he answered,

"I am surprised that you even care, Cuz. What's this? Am I to understand that you actually believe me now after all this time?"

"Just answer the question." He answered irritated by his heir.

"No, I have not had any other run-ins with dubious characters, if that is what you mean."

Sebastian walked over to the table and poured the two of them a brandy, handing one to Darcy while downing his in one go, before refilling his glass. Darcy studied him as his cousin appeared deep in thought. Something was wrong, so he waited patiently for whatever he wished to tell him, knowing that it would eventually come. His patience was rewarded.

"I need to tell you something, and I must say that I am surprising myself as you are the last person I would have anticipated having this conversation with, believe me."

He continued cautiously, telling him of the attempts on his own life and his suspicions that the deaths of his whole family were no accident. Darcy's look of utter astonishment would have been amusing had it not been for the seriousness underlying his cousin's every word.

"I thought it was you who was responsible for the attempts on my life and I married to beget an heir before anything else might happen," the duke explained. "It was my men who came to your aid on the first occasion you were assaulted. I have had you watched closely for a number of weeks now." Sebastian took another sip of his brandy while Darcy sunk himself into a nearby chair. Utter silence ensued while both men thought of events in the past.

Darcy looked up at his cousin.

"So I have you to thank for saving my life." He was finding it difficult to come to terms with everything he had just heard. It still seemed incredible that the duke who had professed hatred for him for so long, was now actually confiding in him. His heart lightened towards this man who had in the last year, shown such malice towards him. His cousin needed his help. That much was evident. He had been through so much.

"I know this, Cuz. I will have to shelve my plans for a certain young lady for a while and you will need to keep a keen eye on your wife if the suspicions you have hold any truth. Her Grace's life could be in great danger if it is someone with their eye on the dukedom, which seems to be the case. If indeed it is someone with an eye on the title, they will not wish her to give birth and produce another heir."

"I have already thought of that. I have forty men around the estate and she will not be allowed to move without someone close by."

"Will you tell her?"

"Good God, no!" Sebastian barked. "I cannot have her worrying about something that I could be completely wrong about. She is better off in ignorance. Until I have something concrete, I don't want anyone else other than Colby, the agent I have hired, and you, to know. I would not have told you but for the fact you need to take great care how you proceed. My men will still follow your every move, mind."

"They cannot stop a bullet, Seb!" Darcy warned calling his cousin by his shortened name for the first time in years, "although I do appreciate your efforts to keep me safe!"

"It is to keep me safe also, believe me." The duke looked grim. "If you should turn out to be the killer, my men will see that you do not inherit if anything untoward happens to me. They would ensure you did not live long enough should that be the case."

"You still think I am the guilty party?" Darcy asked, astonished by his cousin's words.

"I did, for a long time………Now I do not know what to believe." Sebastian said. "It is rather daunting not knowing who your enemy is or where he may turn up next."

Both men sat deep in thought for a while, but it was Darcy that appeared to come to a decision first.

"I think I will stay here for a while, Cuz. You may have your people prepare me a suite of rooms. I intend to get to the bottom of this and two heads are better than one."

"There is no need for that!" Sebastian said.

"There is every need." Darcy replied. "You need my help more than you know."
"People will wonder why you stay here when I am supposed to be on my honeymoon."

"Damn people. We need to comb through every bit of information you can get your hands on and we can do it better here. This is where your first wife died. If you are correct in your suspicions, then someone looking like me infiltrated this house and pushed Dulcie to her death. We need to start first with that information."

Sebastian eyed him curiously then rang for a maid.

"You are correct. I will have a suite of rooms made up for you, and Darcy,………… not a word to my wife. You may tell her you are rusticating because you have gone through your allowance gambling and womanising."

Darcy gave out a sudden bark of laughter. "By jove, you love making me out to be the rake."

"Trust me, she will believe it more easily than that you cannot tear yourself away from me. She must not know of our latest scrape." His face suddenly softened. He paused, deep in thought.

"How Andrew would have loved to have solved this mystery."

At that moment, a maid entered and was given the necessary instructions to prepare rooms and light a fire for Lord Darcy. The maid tried to hide her surprise as she looked from one man to the other, but failed miserably while bowing herself out.

Come, My wife awaits me." Sebastian said as he clapped Darcy on the back. They walked out together, both feeling pleased and relieved that they had ceased hostilities for the time, at least.

Chapter Six

As he entered the drawing room, his eyes were once again drawn to his wife. Inwardly he seethed at the thought that she had tricked him. Pretending to be a plain Jane when she was a stunning young woman! Suddenly, she looked across at him and gave him a dazzling smile of welcome. His insides did a somersault. He watched her turn towards his friends as one of them asked her something. She answered him smiling, then after excusing herself, walked gracefully towards her aunt.

After a while, she stood up in readiness to take her leave of the company. The guests simultaneously raised a glass to her as she left accompanied by her aunt and her cousin. Sebastian watched as they left the room together. Once again he seethed inwardly. His aunt had been an accomplice. She had played him for a fool. His thoughts ran to his wife.

She had given little of her attention to him, yet now she belonged to him body and soul. He glanced at the clock on the mantle longing for the time to fly, so that he could start to school her in the correct behaviour conducive to his duchess.

Meanwhile, upstairs, his wife, Arabella was preparing herself for her new husband while her godmother reluctantly took her leave of her.

"My dear, I am sure he is besotted! Never have I seen him look so annoyed when I demanded his attention. While all his cronies were paying you court, he was positively jealous, I do believe."

"Oh no, I am sure he was merely tired of the whole façade. He does not like to socialise, you know. Don't forget Aunt, ours is not a love match. Ours is a marriage of convenience."

Arabella had to keep reminding herself of this fact.

Her aunt would have none of it, however.

"His dislike of witnessing his beautiful new wife basking in the attention of his friends was a pleasure to behold. I vow I have not seen him so filled with emotion since……………well, let us just say, I have not seen him filled with emotion for a long time." Her godmother strolled across the room, hugging herself and laughing merrily.

"My dear, the truth is, he did not see you as a beauty when we played you down before you were wed. Now his eyes are opened he is bound to fall in love with you. I knew it would work."

"But I only agreed to new clothes and hairstyle to please him and not disgrace him in any way."

Lady Peabody clapped her hands and looked towards the heavens,

"And now you have blossomed into a beauty and he will not be able to resist you."

"If that were only so, but I do believe, he sees beauty as a threat."

"My dear, be yourself, and he will eventually see beauty not only from the outside, but from the inside," and with this she gave her god daughter a kiss and left the room leaving her in the capable hands of her maid, Molly.

****

Arabella stood nervously facing him in her diaphanous night-rail, aware that he could see through to her burning skin. The guests had departed hours ago and she had patiently waited for his arrival.

Oh God, he was such a handsome specimen she thought, but she must never allow him to see how physically attracted she was to him. His pristine, white shirt emphasised his bronzed skin and dark hair that for once, hung loose to his shoulders. Strange how he didn't conform to the fashionably short styles men wore. He was a man with his own mind and tastes and would never follow others. He would always lead. She liked that in him.

He strolled towards her never taking his eyes off her face, slowly studying the flowing creation she had worn for him. It pleased him that she had donned something provocative for him on this night, but he could not rid himself of the feeling that she wanted more than he was willing to give. He would soon disabuse her of that notion. Perhaps he was still in shock since the first moment he had witnessed her walk down the aisle taking her place beside him. He still felt a burning anger that she had tricked him, playing down her beauty, instead of flaunting it in the sure knowledge that he would be lulled into a false sense of security.

Women were all jades and false to the core. Why should this one be any different? I will need to be on my guard!

His eyes raked her body, noticing how her breasts peaked through the thin material. His breathing became laboured as he succumbed to his earthy desires. She was his to do with as he wished. He was racked by both desire and anger towards her and furious that he had little control where she was concerned.

She stood looking the picture of innocence yet her reaction to his friends had shown a lack of maidenly decorum on her part. Surely, a virgin would have shied away from their comments which he was sure were meant to put her to the blush. Instead, she had laughed with them. Moreover, her laugh was earthy and sexier than any other woman he had ever known; a level of laughter she had yet to share with him. How dare she play the whore in front of his friends and family. They would know her for what she was and once again a woman would shame him. He could not allow that to happen.

An urge to punish her for all the lecherous looks she had received from his friends urged him to take her this minute without mercy. The jade had openly flirted at the reception, smiling and encouraging their lascivious words. He knew his friends well. Dulcie had encouraged men. Many men. Just how many men had lain with her he did not know to this day. He would not be made to look the fool again. Arabella would learn from the start that he was in control of this relationship. He reached out and slid his fingers around the neckline of her night-rail.

"Take it off," he demanded, looking into those seemingly innocent eyes.

All women were actresses, he thought, as she slowly disrobed.

He watched her as her hands trembled as she undid the ribbons that held the delectable creation together.

"Are you cold?" He sneered not believing for one moment that she was the innocent she portrayed. God, he was angry with her. He could not imagine how he had come to deserve another Dulcie, but he would keep this one so satisfied that she would not have the energy to go looking further afield for more. He would ensure she was satiated every time he took her and the way he was feeling, it would be often. He had enough to think about with the identity of a murderer without worrying about another woman.

Her long dark hair fell in glorious waves to the centre of her back and he ran it through his fingers as she stood naked before him; her whole body quivering as he traced a line from her throat to her breast bone.

"Understand me when I say you are mine, madam, to do with as I wish. From now on what I tell you to do, you will do." His voice was husky and it sent quivers through her.

His eyes raked her body, and she burned all over.

"I will not hurt you but I intend to have all of you and you will submit to my desires as a wife should. Do you understand me?"

"I do," she replied, still quivering from his touch. "I am your wife."

Oh God, why was he so angry?

The thought that she had already displeased him in some way, filled her with trepidation. "I really do wish to please you, your Grace."

He moved closer to her mouth and she could feel his breath on her face.

"As long as we understand each other!" It was merely a whisper on her cheek but her insides began to throb with a desire that she did not understand. Arabella was frightened but tried not to show it. She knew she was not afraid of Sebastian, only of what was before her. No-one had explained to her how to make babies, but she knew that she had to submit to her husband because her aunt had said that she was to follow his lead in all things and that she would be alright.

Lady Peabody adored Sebastian and she was a good judge of character. Arabella knew that she would not have suggested marriage to him if she had not thought that they would find some happiness together and instinctively she knew that he was a good man who cared for his people.

She trusted him. Her godmother trusted him. That was enough to allow her to surrender to his will. She breathed deeply in an attempt to curb her fear of the unknown. Suddenly, he picked her up and strode to the bed, laying her on the mattress and following her down.

"Your Grace," she said, as he still had not given her permission to use his name, "are you not going to get undressed?"

"Never mind me," he replied. "I intend to know you this evening so just lie back and let me look at you. Tonight I will make you mine."

He trailed a finger slowly down her body devouring her with his eyes until he reached that most private part of her. She knew she blushed as he gently caressed her intimately, touching a part that made her whole body tense then her innermost core seemed to spiral into a delicious sensation that made her want him to touch her there again. She felt ashamed of her feelings and did not understand them. Her fingers itched to touch him but he would not let her, gently pushing her hands away.

He continued to move down her legs with his hands, even moving himself to reach her lower legs and feet, then her toes sending inflammatory feelings everywhere. She wanted him to touch her intimately again but his hands moved towards her breast and circled the tip until it stood out erect causing sensations throughout her body. Instinctively, she moved closer towards him.

He gently pushed her back and bent to her nipple and suckled it until she cried out. The lower half of her body seemed to have a mind of its own, moving, needing to be in closer contact with him.

What is happening to me? she thought as she squirmed, and continued to move her lower body as he caressed one breast and suckled the other.

God, this is wonderful, she thought, as his hands slowly moved down to her hips and then to her private parts. She let out a sigh of ecstasy. He touched her in that sensitive part that prior to this evening, she never knew existed, but which she slowly realised, could give her exquisite pleasure.

He continued to touch and circle that special place and the feeling almost drove her crazy with desire for more, yet she did not know what she craved. All she knew was that she needed more. A hollow feeling started to build within her core. As she writhed to the unrelenting pressure of his fingers on her special place she felt out of control.

Her whole body pushed itself towards him. As the feelings intensified, her hips moved up and down unconsciously, faster and faster until the pressure built so much she was tensing her buttocks and suddenly she gained some sort of release from the pressure that was the most vibrant feeling she had ever encountered in her life. She cried out unable to suppress the sensations he was arousing inside of her.

This feeling continued to grow and expand until she felt she was going to explode and suddenly, a strange liquid released itself from her core and she rode along with it until it slowly dissipated, leaving her replete and floating.

She lay for a while catching her breath as she became aware of Sebastian's gaze upon her. She smiled gently at him so grateful for the pleasure he aroused inside of her. She felt that he had transported her to somewhere like heaven.

Perhaps theirs would become a happy marriage after all if this was anything to go by.

"Thank you," she said, thinking that was the end of the goings on between a man and a woman to create a baby but not quite understanding how it happened like that.

"We have not finished yet," he said, looking at her lips as she tried to slow her breathing.

She slowly traced her tongue around her lower lip as she was feeling quite dry, but suddenly, his mouth was on hers, forcing hers to open and his tongue was invading her mouth causing such havoc she again felt that strange liquid running from her insides down in her private region. His kiss was all that she could ever want and she had never imagined how intimate and delectable that it could feel. It took her breath away while again she wished to push closer to his body.

She clawed at his shirt wishing to feel him naked next to her but he gently pushed her hands away and once again while continuing to devour her mouth touched her in that intimate part that sent her writhing and bucking and wanting so much more of something elusive. His other hand was kneading her breast while his fingers continued to caress the special place that sent her into ecstasy. She felt as though she was losing her mind, all will to do anything but writhe underneath this man and feel the wonderful feelings he aroused in her.

God, can I stand anymore of this without my whole body exploding? She gave herself up to the brand new feelings that engulfed her.

Suddenly, she became aware of Sebastian moving and fumbling with his garments but was unsure what he had been doing until a hot, hard rod was pushing into her, replacing his fingers which had given her so much pleasure. It felt rather large and her whole body stiffened and she screamed as he moved himself hard into her, causing a burning sensation to permeate through her lower regions. It stilled her writhing and she froze for a few minutes as she came to terms with his huge member resting inside her after the initial pain.

This is what makes a baby, and I do not like this part she thought until suddenly the hard member inside her started slowly moving in and out and repeating the slow rhythm until she started feeling that strange yearning for it to go deeper and deeper. Suddenly it stopped and she opened her eyes not realising that she had closed them through these strange sensations which were all so very new to her. She stared up into his fathomless eyes and then noticed concern in them.

"Are you all right? You need to stop me if you are not." he asked, seemingly staring into her very soul.

She nodded, continuing to slowly move her hips and suddenly he let out a deep growl and continued to move inside her deeper and deeper until she seemed to have all of him. Never would she have imagined him capable of pushing in to her that deeply and still pushing deeper. She was bucking and writhing and moaning and screaming and so filled that her insides felt as though they were taken over by him; as if they were one person seemingly joined forever in these glorious sensations that suddenly spiralled into a huge vortex of shooting stars, rippling waves and gushing geezers and then a volcanic eruption that found her opening and releasing her very soul to him. It was as if their souls were one and always would be for ever and eternity.

It was a long time before she became aware of the world around her and suddenly, as she slowly opened her eyes, Sebastian was staring at her, not with the love and the bond and the enormous feeling of oneness that she had experienced, but with a look of horror that intensified as she focussed upon him. She smiled, shyly, knowing that something special had happened between them but not understanding why he was seemingly angry with her. Her smile faded abruptly.

I have failed. I have not pleased him.

Slowly, she realised, he was speaking to her.

"I beg your pardon?" she replied, shyly.

"I said, I will leave you to sleep now, but be prepared for me to take you where and when I choose. You will not leave this house unless you ask my permission in case I have need of you at any given time of the day or night."

A cold chill pervaded her body at his cruel words. All the euphoria of the past hour dissipated and she felt as if he had thrown cold water over her face. What was she guilty of, for heaven's sake? She had tried so hard to give him her all. Perhaps she was just not enough.

How can he talk to me like this after we have experienced such perfect bliss together? How can he think he can make me a prisoner?

She could not understand him but even when he hurt her so badly, she sensed that he needed her in some way and for the moment, she was willing to go along with his demands as long as he did not harm her. It hurt that he obviously failed to share the sensations that she had, but she was still grateful enough to him for making her feel so beautiful and loved and worshiped for a small amount of time at least and for the gift of the very new sensations that she had never known existed.

"Goodnight, your Grace." she said coldly, trying most desperately to hide the hurt that he would not sleep with her and sought his own room on this of all nights. He had made it clear that she was a brood mare that he wished to use, but she was also honest enough to admit to herself that she was using him for her desire for children so he was as much of a stallion to her as she was the tool for his heir. She must keep reminding herself that theirs was not a love match. Theirs was a marriage of mutual convenience.

The trouble was, she had not realised how much pleasure there was in the art of love making and how much she would look forward to the next time her virile husband sought his husbandly rights. She lay awake for hours, recalling his words and facing the enigma that was the duke.

He didn't care for her as his speedy departure from her bed proved, but then, she had known that he did not love her.

How difficult this was.

She now wondered if he had felt anything when he had entered her. His breathing seemed to grow rapid and he had groaned a little towards the end, but he had quickly regained his equilibrium, at least far faster than she had. Had he merely entered her bedroom tonight because he had a duty towards the dukedom? She had to keep reminding herself that men could perform this act anytime with any woman and not feel affection towards them.

Her father had many mistresses and had never felt anything for them or else he would not have left them so often. They fulfilled his needs and his male urges. That was how her maid, Molly had explained it. Her maid knew about these things because she had a sister who had strayed and was now a fallen woman in the eyes of Molly's family. Except for Molly, they had turned their backs on her sister when they had discovered she was no better than she ought to be. She was now a kept woman.

Perhaps this is how the duke felt towards her. She was a means to an end. His desire was for an heir and a spare. She had no value other than her body. He was only telling the truth when he said that she belonged to him body and soul.

She would try to be an obedient wife although the thought gave her pause for thought. She was no better than Molly's sister.

The title duchess meant nothing to her, except for the responsibilities she had inherited that were important to her. More people relied upon her now. As much as she wanted to please him, she did not intend to follow her mother's path. She would not stand back and pretend her husband was being faithful and that all was right with the world.

If he strayed, she would leave him even though she knew he was the only man she could ever wish to have in her bed. During the early hours of the morning, she drifted off to sleep, to dream of her elusive, complicated husband.

Chapter Seven

Meanwhile, Sebastian walked the floor of his bedroom in the early hours, anticipating another visit to his wife first thing in the morning.

He was terrified by the feelings this woman created in him. Merely to remember her perfectly soft skin stirred his member. He wanted her now and the thought filled him with terror. How could a woman generate such feelings of lust inside him after only one hour of love making? He was consumed with the emotions she had aroused in him. He resented feeling as he did at this moment.

There was something about her that stirred him every time he thought of her. He felt trapped. He did not wish to feel anything for her. She was there to produce heirs, nothing more. And yet….. her innocent demeanour; her wish to please……..There were so many things he liked about her. Perhaps it was her voice that was so gentle and melodious. Or perhaps, his baser side thought it was her delectable body. Dulcie had been beautiful, but he had to be honest to himself and admit, she had not aroused the feelings in him that Arabella did without effort. He found this difficult to understand.

She had been so compliant and then a willing partner, wanting to give as well as take. Dulcie had never given anything after she had been married for six months. Indeed, she had been compliant but not overly interested in the physical side of their marriage. Then again, he knew she had strayed, making a mockery of their relationship. The thought of Arabella straying pierced him deeply. He would not be able to cope with betrayal again, particularly from his new wife. No, he would keep her satiated. That was the only way.

Thoughts of his first wife brought anger to the fore. He had blamed himself until he realised that there were so many others sharing her favours.

It would not happen again. He would ensure that Arabella had eyes only for him. She belonged to him and now he knew she was a willing partner, he would keep her that way. He would teach her so much. Hardly a hardship!

****

She slowly became aware of him as she awoke to such exquisite feelings. He was touching her body, and lazily, still half asleep, she opened her legs wide to accommodate him in any way he wished.

"Good morning, Your Grace," she said in a husky voice, smiling up at him.

"Good morning, Your Grace," he whispered in her ear as he touched her more intimately, jolting her fully awake. "I want you, now." He said, as he moved on top of her and thrust himself inside her.

It was painful for only a moment as she was still not as ready for him as she would have liked but even the pain was somehow a pleasure. She wanted him inside her; was glad that he had crept into her bed, and even more glad that he really appeared to desire her. Gone was the anger of last evening. She burned wherever he touched.

He moved inside her and she felt as though she was overwhelmed with this man who thrust so forcefully almost in desperation. She tried to open herself more and more to accommodate his large member and eventually was swallowed up by her own desire to reach that climax that her body seemed so desperate to claim. Rapidly, they both spiralled together totally out of control.

It was a few minutes before either of them could speak but once they had both regained their composure, Arabella looked into his eyes and once again realised they were shuttered and somehow formidable. Moreover, she was aware in that instant that he was again, fully clothed.

What is he hiding from me?

The thought hurt that he could take her body which she would give willingly, but would not share his when it was her dearest wish. She did not dare to say anything about it lest he become angry with her, but could not understand why he did not undress in the same way that she had for him. Molly had told her that men and women lay naked together.

What is wrong with me? Does he despise me so much?

He did not depart promptly like he had the night before.

As she lay on her back with her nightgown half way up her body, he demanded that she take it off. This she did, hoping that he would take off his clothes as well so she could feel his skin next to hers. Perhaps that would come naturally when he felt he could trust her.

He lay there his hands roaming over her as she lay satiated. She felt so relaxed after their lovemaking that she did not care what he did to her. At this moment in time, she knew she would obey him in everything.

She watched him closely as he traversed her body with his hands, causing havoc wherever he lingered. He suckled her breasts and her lower regions throbbed for his attention.

She became liquid in his hands and could not prevent the sheer moan of delight as he touched her in that private place. He slowly increased the pressure as she writhed, transported into relentless pleasure. How she wanted him inside her thrusting and reaching that ultimate part of her that exploded into atoms. He continued the pressure and sent her into mindlessness. He seemed in no immediate hurry to join with her as she reached the climax that engulfed her, laying shuddering in his arms.

Suddenly, when she thought it was all over, he rolled on top of her and opening his trousers, he thrust inside her hard and fast so that she caught her breath. He continued a punishing rhythm that found her meeting him at every thrust. She tried to relax, so that he could bury himself deep inside her and then she felt him shudder and slowly cease to move further.

He lay there replete, not wanting to separate from this woman that held him enthralled sexually. Not any one of his mistresses had aroused such feelings in him and yet an innocent bride had achieved it. He would never let her go. It frightened him just how possessive he felt towards this woman. He wanted to lock her up and keep her solely for his pleasure even though he knew he should not feel this way. Surely, he would eventually tire of her. He hoped so as he could not afford to feel this vulnerable. Surely a type of madness had come over him. He was deeply ashamed.

Even now, he wished to stay in bed with her. He had elected to keep his clothes on as he could not totally open to her. It was a form of protection. The thought of being naked with her inflamed him but he resisted it, sure that if he did, he would not be able to control himself. These feelings were too raw and even with this pathetic attempt at protection, he already knew that it was not working. He would try, though because her power over him scared him almost witless.

Perhaps if he just kept her satiated, she would not look to others for fulfilment. He needed to be close to her and the thought grew ever more powerful as he stroked her soft skin. He would strive desperately to mask his feelings in front of her for sure. He drove into her more aroused than he had ever been and yet she met him at every turn. Her body arched perfectly to accommodate his as though she anticipated every move he made. He thrust deeply again and again, totally lost in her yet she never murmured, merely moving in unison with him until she climaxed and he spilled his seed inside her.

Gasping for breath, he was angered to think that she had been so innocently in control of him rather than the other way around and he knew this had to stop. He had to leave this room immediately. He would teach her to be compliant and servile instead of arousing him to such a degree that he could not control his feelings. She would learn, by God she would. He roused himself enough to exit the bed and walked away from her without a word.

That would teach her. She would learn her place!

But as he stormed from the bedroom, guilt at the thought that he had probably hurt her consumed him.

Where were his wits with this woman? Had he become an animal?

He felt he had let himself down. Initially, he had questioned her virginity. He had been wrong about that. She was an innocent. Should he trust her? Did all women pose a threat when they became too close? He felt so vulnerable.

I need to resume control.

The worst thing was, at this present moment, he did not know how he could do it. He would go to his study to think things through. It was the only place he felt was his own private domain in this entire building.

He thought back to his first marriage. From the start, the Hall had been given over to Dulcie whose opulent taste in all things had given him a distaste of the interior of the whole building. The study had remained his only private domain other than his bedroom. Her suite of rooms was next to his, but since her death, he had not entered it and neither had anyone else except her maid. He supposed he should have it redecorated for Arabella, but he would allow her to decide whether she wished to take over the Duchess Suite as it was named. Perhaps he would discuss this after breakfast!

If she did, his problem would be having her so close every night. How could he lie in his bed at night knowing she was only a few yards away? He told himself that he felt more secure with her in the east wing which was a long way from his own suite of rooms.

Just who am I trying to convince?

His thoughts turned to the last twelve months. Distasteful memories had prevented him from returning to Huxton Hall. It was his nearest estate to London and, if he was lucky, someone would remember something. Perhaps it would lead them to the person who was trying to wipe out his entire family. It seemed so unbelievably extreme. The more he thought about it, the more sure he became that there was someone who wanted to destroy the whole dynasty of Winslow. Just who would want this so much that they would ruthlessly kill innocent people? The thought sent a chill up through his spine. He took a deep breath and let out a long sigh. He could still be barking up the wrong tree.

I don't want this problem. After all I have been through in the last few years, why must I have to deal with something like this, now?

For a moment, the thought filled him with self-pity, but then his thoughts turned to a time when his life had been so totally different. Looking back he could remember when he felt truly happy and secure. Andrew had been alive then. His twin! Someone whom he could always rely upon. They had been so close. It was a time when Darcy had been a staunch friend to both of them.

He smiled to himself as he thought back to the days that were full of innocent mischief. The days when they galloped over the fields and waged friendly bets; where they enjoyed going to house parties and building stables second to none. In those days, Sebastian believed he had been born lucky and yet, for the last five years, he had been stripped of all his family. All of the people he loved most in the world. There was now only himself and Darcy who after Dulcie's death, he had truly believed had betrayed him.

But perhaps, if his supposition was true, it was what he was supposed to believe. What better way to depose an heir than to make him out to be a scoundrel! Could it be that Darcy was set up in the hope that Sebastian would call him out? He shuddered at the thought; looking back, it had almost happened.

Only the responsibility towards his family had prevented him from doing such a thing. First, he did not desire to kill his heir even though he had hated him at that time. Second, he did not wish for an even bigger scandal than the ones that Dulcie had already created.

All this time, he had felt out of control of the events in his life. It was time to face up to his problems and discover just who was threatening him and the life of his heir. He would cease being a victim and leave no stone unturned until he found the culprit and put a stop to the evil that was threatening any happiness for the future.

Chapter Eight

"The staff seem quite miserable, your Grace." Molly stated as she brushed Arabella's hair. "They are quite close mouthed and hardly speak to me."

"Why do you think that is, Molly? Is it because they see me as a usurper?"

Perhaps they believe I am not worthy to take the place of his Grace's first wife!

The thought filled her with trepidation.

"I am not sure, your Grace."

"Oh, cease calling me, your Grace," Arabella implored, feeling exasperated. "You have been my maid for years and I need a friend in this house. 'My lady' will do very well Molly, unless we are in company."

"As you wish, my lady." Molly replied, and curtseyed as a matter of habit more than deference. She loved her mistress but was glad that they would still continue the relationship that they had enjoyed since she became her maid when her ladyship was the tender age of fifteen. She was pleased that they would still share a bond of friendship even though she was now a duchess. Molly would do anything for her as she adored her.

"I will try to discover their true feelings below stairs, my lady. I do believe that there are a couple I could befriend if I stay out of the beady eyes of Mrs Hobbs, the housekeeper. She is so stern! She makes me quake in my shoes, she does." Molly stared into thin air and shuddered as if trying to erase a disquieting vision in her mind.

"I would be pleased if you could apprise me of the mood downstairs as the days go by. It is early yet and we must have patience. It is important that we do not create hostilities as it has only been just over a year since his

Grace's first wife died. They must feel the loss as he does." Arabella exclaimed.

"As to that, my lady, I am sure you must speak the truth as Briany, as was her Grace's maid, still looks after her rooms next to his Grace's and will let no-one enter, even to clean. Does it all herself. The under housemaid Jeanie told me, though she's tried to enter on occasion."

Arabella looked askance, her almond eyes widening, slightly.

"Are you saying that no-one has entered her rooms since she has died?" Arabella queried, amazed that this should be so. Surely her husband would have the suite redecorated now in preparation for his new duchess.

"According to Jeanie, the under housemaid, Briany is something of a tyrant and even Mrs Hobbs is scared of her temper. There are whisperings that the room is haunted and that her Grace as they still calls her haunts the rooms and they're all scared to enter."

"What utter nonsense!" Arabella stated, "And what does his Grace say to all of this?"

"Why nothing, my lady as word is that he will not enter her rooms as his heart is broken and he can't bear to go near them……….Oh! I'm sorry if I have offended you, my lady."

"Nonsense, Molly. You do not offend me in the least……………. He must have loved her very much. I do believe, however, that I will visit the rooms to see for myself if they are haunted or not."

Besides the fact that I wish to see what the rooms look like and discover for myself if there is anything that I can do to lessen his Grace's grief. Perhaps I can have them re-decorated and stripped of all the items that would constantly remind him of her!……

"You can go now," Arabella said, "but please tell Mrs Hobbs that I wish to see her in the Blue Room after I have breakfasted. I noticed it yesterday and think that I will make it my own. It appears the least offensive that I have seen so far."

"Yes, my lady. I will tell her at once."

As Arabella walked into the large, ornate breakfast parlour, her eyebrows rose in surprise at the sight of Lord Rutherford and her new husband in what appeared to be a serious, but very quiet conversation.

Both men who were leaning towards each other, somewhat oblivious to anything else, suddenly sat upright and then stood as she made her way to the table. She noticed a frown quickly disappear from his Grace's face as his eyes held hers as she took her place at the table.

"Your Grace, good morning," Lord Rutherford bowed, his warm smile, ever present, creasing his face.

"Would you like to sit here?" Sebastian offered as he pulled out the chair that was next to his own on the opposite side of the long table from Lord Rutherford.

She bowed her head in agreement and made her way to the seat offered to her, instead of the one she had originally chosen a little further down the table. She was pleased that she did not have to sit at the opposite end to her husband as the table had at least twenty leaves, which would have made conversation impossible.

She made a mental note to ensure that the table was either greatly reduced in future or another much smaller table arranged in a prominent, light position to catch the early morning sunshine.

"Thank you, your Grace." She replied and turning towards Lord Rutherford said, "I am surprised to see you here. Will you be staying with us for long?"

He cleared his throat, thoughtfully considering her question before answering,

"My stay at present is indefinite, your Grace. I hope you do not mind."

Arabella looked from her husband to his heir in utter confusion. It was his Grace that eventually offered an explanation.

"Darcy finds himself needing to rusticate for the time being, my dear, so he can be of assistance to me with the running of the estates." She glanced between the men. Somehow she was not quite convinced that this was the precise reason for Lord Rutherford's presence but forbore to disclose that she did not believe him.

There was a mystery here. She had thought that the two men had much enmity between them but now it did not seem to be the case. It was, however, none of her concern so she could dismiss her feelings of doubt completely.

Instead, she turned to Lord Rutherford and smiled amiably, saying, "My Lord, you are more than welcome. I hope you enjoy your stay with us."

Lord Rutherford's grey eyes warmed considerably. "I am grateful to your Grace." Was all he replied.

"I don't see the need to stay on ceremony when we are the three of us." Sebastian declared, "You may call my wife by her given name" and as he turned to Arabella, he said, "For God's sake woman, call me either Somerville or Seb. Your choice!"

Arabella's heart swelled as she felt a door had been opened to further intimacy albeit his given name. She was so grateful for this crumb, she bowed her head in acknowledgement and accepted coddled eggs off the footman who served her from a tray.

A warm, secret smile played over her face. She felt that the sun was indeed shining on her today. They conversed pleasantly about the wedding and those who had attended, when they were likely to meet again and just how successful the day's celebrations were. The men did not linger at the table, excusing themselves when Arabella had finished her coffee.

"I will send Mrs Hobbs into you, my dear and she can show you around. Please feel free to redecorate or change anything you wish. You have carte blanche to do whatever you would like to make this a home."

Once again, her eyelids rose in surprise, but this would give her the authority she required to make the changes she felt were in dire need. She smiled at her husband in gratitude and was thrilled when his own blue eyes lit up in what she felt was either appreciation or satisfaction.

At least she felt he was no longer angry with her. Her heart warmed towards him and her whole body began to tremble at the remembered intimacies they had shared the previous night and early this morning. She looked forward in anticipation to the next time he took her to bed. Again, her whole body quivered and realising what was happening, she quickly looked up at the footmen through a guilty haze, grateful that he was not looking her way. She had to take control of her feelings. This would never do. It was with a secret smile and with a feeling of guilty pleasure that she met Mrs Hobbs who would show her around Huxton Hall. Life as the Duchess of Somerville had its good moments.

****

Arabella could understand how the servants would find Mrs Hobbs to be a formidable lady to work for. About average height, she was a little on the plump side, a chiselled face with grey hair tied tightly in a bun that emphasised the severity of her features. There appeared to be no compromise in the older lady. She had an air of continual disapproval that in any other person than Arabella might quell all feelings of pleasure and happiness.

As she curtseyed her features did not change or yield even the slightest of smiles. Fortunately, as the daughter of an Earl and with many years of experience managing staff, Arabella knew just how to run a household. In her experience, you gained more out of servants if they were happy and a dour faced housekeeper was unacceptable.

"Good morning Mrs Hobbs," Arabella said in a brisk voice. "Please to be seated." The woman rather grudgingly did as she was bid but looked as though she would prefer to be anywhere other than with her new mistress.

"Tell me, Mrs Hobbs, do you enjoy your position as housekeeper here in the Hall?" The lady looked nonplussed and slightly uncomfortable about the question. Arabella thought that she actually squirmed in her seat at Arabella's words.

"I do not know what you mean, your Grace," she said. "I have always tried to serve his Grace and he has found no fault in me." She stated, obviously resenting Arabella's tone. "You don't know what I has to put up with, being new to taking the place of the late duchess as it were."

"But that is not what I asked you," Arabella answered quietly,

"I merely wish to ascertain if you enjoy your position or is there something bothering you that we need to discuss. I am of the opinion that the Hall could do with a few changes, and foremost must be to ensure it is a happy place in which to work."

Once again the housekeeper looked decidedly uncomfortable.

"As to that, your Grace, it has not been long since his Grace's first wife died and there are those in this house that still mourn her loss."

"And you are one of them?" Arabella asked sympathetically, feeling at that moment as though she had a mountain to climb.

"Oh no, your Grace. I mean, that is, well, her Grace was not the easiest of people; but I should not speak ill of the dead." Mrs Hobbs visibly squirmed.

"I need to know just how things stand, Mrs Hobbs and it is not helpful if you cannot be candid with me." Arabella said in exasperation.

"While it is very sad that her Grace died so tragically, life must go on. We cannot move forwards if we are forever looking backwards. If his Grace can move forward, then so must the staff that serve him."

Mrs Hobbs brightened considerably for a few seconds until a wayward thought caused the return of her dour expression once more.

"I do agree with you, your Grace and during the time when his Grace's mother was the duchess, the place was filled with happiness." A fond smile passed over Mrs Hobbs's face as she recalled treasured memories. It noticeably transformed her face into a softer, more relaxed person.

"That was when the twins, or begging your pardon, his Grace and his brother were growing up." The Hall was always filled with laughter, but there have been so many tragedies in the last few years."

"All the more reason to move forwards and create happy times, Mrs Hobbs. I mean it when I say that I wish the Hall to be a happy place to work. You must decide whether to move forwards with me or be left behind. I cannot have a housekeeper who is not of the same mind as myself. Now are you with me in this or do you wish to leave the Hall?"

A look of sheer fear engulfed Mrs Hobbs. Although it was uncomfortable and against her nature to cause another's pain, Arabella knew that if she was to change things, she had to make a firm stand from the beginning. She watched closely as a myriad of emotions flew across the housekeeper's face. There was a pregnant pause before the housekeeper's whole demeanour altered and she answered,

"You asked me to be truthful with you, your Grace and I suppose after your last words, I haven't got much to lose." Arabella's face retained its smile.

"Your Grace," she began hesitatingly, "above all I wish to move forwards with you. I would be that glad to see the place brought back to what it once was, but there is one who is stopping it from happening and she has the whole staff including myself at her mercy. Please believe me when I say the staff used to be happy here but when her Grace or her late Grace as she is now married his Grace, she brought with her a viper who has poisoned everything and everyone working here."

Mrs Hobbs had recourse to a handkerchief which she had pulled out from the pocket of her apron as she had spoken. She blew her nose rather loudly and Arabella was surprised to see tears in the older lady's eyes. The housekeeper looked around as though the walls had ears then continued in a quiet voice just above a whisper all the while scanning the room in case anyone should hear her words.

"Please believe me, your Grace, for what I has to say is the truth. I swear before God as is my witness that I have not done anything wrong but she has threatened to tell his Grace all kinds of wickedness about me if I don't do as she says and let her do as she likes. She has the whole staff under her evil spell and everyone is that scared."

Again, Mrs Hobbs blew her nose and wiped her eyes and Arabella could see that the housekeeper was genuinely distressed.

"One moment, Mrs Hobbs, let us make ourselves more comfortable."

Arabella rang for a footman and when he arrived, she ordered tea for two. She was determined to get to the bottom of this besides feeling her own dismay at her harsh behaviour and mistaken estimation of Mrs Hobbs. It was unlike her to jump to conclusions in such a peremptory fashion. After tea was served, Arabella poured and then when Mrs Hobbs had pulled herself together she asked her to begin at the beginning and tell her everything.

The housekeeper was only too pleased to be able to offload the weight she had been carrying around for so long. It appeared that the maid, Briany had been blackmailing Mrs Hobbs and other members of staff and all were afraid of her. The housekeeper explained how she had free reign of the Duchess Suite and no-one was allowed to enter as they feared what evil she might say about them to his Grace. Even the butler was fearful in case she told lies about him.

Admittedly, Mrs Hobbs said, they were accustomed to help themselves liberally on occasion to a bottle of port now and again, but that was the only thing that the Duke was unaware of. Arabella was disposed to disagree on this point and secretly believed that the Duke was well aware of the behaviour of butlers in general.

She had often witnessed her own butler and housekeeper sharing a bottle of port or wine when she had ventured down to the servant's quarters of a summer's evening as a young girl. It was accepted as a normal practice if indeed a right, in many fine houses.

"Why have you allowed this woman to cause so much trouble, Mrs Hobbs? Surely his Grace would have believed your version rather than that of a maid. You have obviously served him for a very long time."

Arabella was absolutely shocked to the core that a mere maid could cause such havoc below stairs. It brought into question the lack of discipline below stairs which would certainly need to be addressed.

"Her mistress always treated her differently from the rest of the staff and she gave her more freedom. She even gifted her with her old clothes. It was as though she was put above all of us. His Grace took no interest in the household. His own mother trusted me with the day to day running of the household but when Briany came to live here, much of this changed."

Mrs Hobbs had recourse to her handkerchief once more, then continued,

I was afraid she would be believed before me, your Grace and she said she would make the maids swear that whatever she said was the truth. They are so scared of her, they would have caved under her threats. I did not wish to lose my position when I have served here for all these years."

"This is beyond belief!" Arabella sympathised, holding her hand out to the woman that still sobbed into her handkerchief.

"Also, his Grace has been so wrapped up in his grief that I could not bring myself to bother him with things I should have been able to deal with myself." Again, she wiped tears from her eyes.

"You must realise your Grace that I have come to despise the woman so much that I have steered clear from her so that I could do my job as best I could. She has put a damper on everything. I am so sorry your Grace. I have failed you all miserably."

Again, Arabella leaned forward and patted the woman's arm in a comforting way.

"Never mind, Mrs Hobbs, do not fear this woman anymore. She will be dealt with, I can promise you."

"Please to be careful, your Grace, she is that evil." Mrs Hobbs warned, fear written all over her face.

"I will," Arabella answered, "now how about a tour of the Hall as soon as you feel more yourself. You may tell me some of its history as we go along," and with that, in a very short space of time, the two women left the blue room together on much more amicable terms.

It became clear to Arabella that the late duchess had spent her days in entertainment and left a great deal of her duties to the housekeeper. After she had ordered each room redecorated in overly bright colours, she had lost interest and had spent her days entertaining or being entertained. Arabella discovered a great deal from the housekeeper who became far more relaxed after unburdening herself to her new mistress.

It appeared that the previous duchess had cared little about the running of the household, but had succumbed to tantrums when things didn't go her way. She had thrown valuable items when in a temper and all the servants had feared her moods, except for Briany her maid who still stayed on now in charge of the Duchess Suite. It was clear that Mrs Hobbs hated her with a vengeance and would have rid herself of her if she didn't hold her in such fear.

As Arabella walked around the rooms, she was pleased to see how clean everything was. The décor, however was over opulent and distasteful. It would appear that Dulcie's taste promoted the use of garish colours that did nothing to lend itself to a restful ambiance and she intuitively felt that Sebastian, as she would now call him, would prefer something a little more quiet. She had discovered that he worked with estate business and often travelled to London to attend the House of Lords and she felt sure that he would much prefer to come home to a restful place.

It would be lovely to see the Hall decorated in pastille colours to ensure a peaceful haven for him whenever her returned from his travels. She would definitely try.

"I will view the Duchess Suite, Mrs Hobbs, but I wish to do so on my own." The housekeeper still looked fearful but guided her to the Suite and left her outside the door. With that, she slowly walked away but with a much lighter step and a smile on her face.

Opening the door, Arabella found the maid reclining on a chaise longue in a deep sleep, a bottle of what looked like gin, on the floor nest to her. Arabella wondered if she was drunk from the night before or had succumbed to the spirits this morning. She had her answer when the woman roused herself after Arabella gave her a nudge in the elbow.

"Go away!" the woman said in a tired rather than a drunken way. Arabella guessed she had stayed up late drinking and did not wish to rouse herself at eleven of the clock.

She stared straight into the woman's eyes that were still bleary from sleep, but were beginning to become more aware every second that went by.

"Briany is your name, I believe?" Arabella asked in a calm tone. At the woman's nod and hasty jerk to her feet, she continued. "Well Briany, you may gather your belongings together and then leave this house immediately. Do I make myself clear?"

Anger, then an intense evil blazed across the maid's face contorting her features. The woman looked like a witch and Arabella could understand how the simple staff at the Hall could live in fear of such a person. Luckily, Arabella was made of sterner stuff.

"You and your like will rue the day you dared to get rid of me!" The maid stated, "I knows things that will destroy you and his nibs. Just wait and see."

Her dark, blurry eyes pierced Arabella's but finding no reaction of fear, slowly searching the area which included the dressing table, then quickly looking elsewhere. Arabella would ensure that she made a thorough search when this woman was gone. To that effect, she strolled towards the bell pull summoning a footman who must have been hovering near the doorway as he entered almost at once.

Mrs Hobbs must have sent him up, bless her!

"You rang your Grace?" the footman intoned, taking in the situation.

"Yes Barnes, is it not?" Arabella smiled, "Could you be so kind as to escort this woman off the Estate immediately and let it be known that she is not to enter it again or I will be calling the magistrate."

The footman beamed, "Yes your Grace. With pleasure, your Grace." He waited for the maid to flounce past Arabella and into the hall.

"Afterwards, Barnes, could you please send Molly to me. I will remain for a while in the Duchess Suite and would like her assistance."

Briany glared and to say her look was murderous was a gross understatement.

After she left escorted dutifully by Barnes, Arabella opened the windows to allow the stench of stale alcohol and sweat to be thoroughly cleansed from the room. It became quiet and peaceful and Arabella imagined the beautiful Lady Dulcie here. It was large and opulent but the colours did not match and as she strolled through the suite of rooms she imagined them re-decorated in softer colours like cream and peach. She peered through the window, thinking that she had never seen such a lovely view.

"My lady, I have found her Grace's diary in the drawer of the dressing table. You may want to look through it."

"Thank you, Molly, but it is not right for me to do that. I will give it to his Grace and he can decide whether he would like to keep it. Meanwhile, could you organise a thorough clean of the full suite and pack away her Grace's belongings."

"Yes, my lady, I will see Mrs Hobbs."

"Thank you, Molly and kindly tell Mrs Hobbs that I do believe that once the curtains were opened, any would be ghosts flew out of the window, so she may like to advise the maids it is quite safe to clean."

The two women smiled at each other in perfect accord.

She was determined to have these rooms refurbished at once and spent the rest of the morning planning just how they would become in a very short space of time. By the end of her first day as the Duchess of Somerville, Arabella was extremely pleased with the developments.

Her housekeeper had become a much happier person. The staff had walked around with huge smiles upon their faces and the ambiance of the whole Hall had miraculously improved. She had caught one of the maids singing as she walked past a bedroom and smiled at her, insisting that she continue with the merry little tune. Even the butler's footsteps appeared lighter as he entered the Blue Room to announce that dinner would be served presently.

Earlier, she had written to Reverend Jonas Althrop of Muchbury, notifying him of her wedding and inviting him to Huxton Hall as she needed to see him about the alterations due to take place in the orphanage. She did not feel easy leaving him with the responsibility but she had yet to find someone who would be suitable. He had advertised for a matron to run the establishment but so far, there had been no real contenders for the position. Perhaps she needed to address the situation herself.

She knew that the board who had been appointed were not really interested in the place, leaving many decisions to her. Something would have to be done about that as she would not have the time in the future to oversee as much as she had before.

During the last two years, she had shouldered much of the responsibility. Althrop was not a good letter writer and had only written to advise her once that all was well.

This did nothing to alleviate her worries and although she arranged the finances from afar, she was concerned about the children's welfare and would prefer to visit in person to see for herself just how the orphanage was running.

She decided that she would arrange a visit for about three months' time. That would give her plenty of time to complete the refurbishment.

The Duke would probably be pleased to have a break from her by then, wouldn't he?

Chapter Nine

Arabella stared at the sky through the window in the library. Once again she had failed him. It had been four very long weeks and he had visited her every night.

She was still shaken over the intense feelings he was able to arouse within minutes with his tender touch. Only last night he had brought her to a state of ecstasy as his hands roamed her body, caressing and stroking and thrilling her to the core. Her body responded to his hands with a mind of its own.

Yet every time he used her, because that was the only way she could now describe it, he would walk away, anger emanating from every pore. She did not know what occurred to cause this and she was too afraid to ask what she had done to displease him. During those other times, she was left to her own devices and attempted to settle into overseeing the day to day running of such a huge household. The decorators had responded promptly and tomorrow they would commence with the decoration of the Duchess Suite. Everything was packed away in the attics except for the diary which was safely tucked away in her bedroom drawer.

Part of her really wished to peep inside to discover more about Dulcie but she felt as though it would be too much of an intrusion. She had meant to pass it over to Sebastian but a part of her wanted it to remain in her possession. *Besides*, she told herself, *it could cause him pain.*

Thoughts of him brought a smile to her face. He had appeared to be pleased with her project to redecorate the Hall in more pastille shades and agreed with the colours much to her surprise. He was always meticulously polite when they met in the dining room but his eyes were shuttered most of the time as though he was hiding something from her. She could not rid herself of the feeling that a line had been drawn between them that she dare not cross.

She kept reminding herself that theirs was a marriage of convenience, but deep down, she knew they could have much more if he would only let her in to heal the pain of Dulcie's passing. Her name was never mentioned and so she respected his reticence, but always, it seemed she was present, coming between them whenever they discussed anything. Sometimes, she wondered if she shared their bed during love making. Did he pretend he had Dulcie writhing under him only to realise it was her; a second best?

Was that what made him angry and resentful towards her? Perhaps Dulcie was the reason he always held back from her, giving but unable to receive anything in return; in effect, shutting her out.

As she surveyed the beautiful landscape before her, she decided it was for the best if she respected his boundaries and launched herself into the responsibilities that were part of being a good duchess.

She decided to have a stroll in the garden even though the wind was easterly and quite fresh. Glancing up, she noticed that fluffy white clouds dappled the sky but the sun was in the process of warming the soil, nurturing the plants which would slowly unfold with tender care. Nature called to her and she responded. She needed to walk in the fresh air and simulate her thoughts after the emotional trauma of the last four weeks. Yes, she would take a walk, just like she was used to do in Muchbury on a fine Spring day.

Her husband was with his agent for the third time since they had married. Arabella was curious as to the conversations they shared which left him morose and unsettled. Indeed her husband's temper and frustration always appeared more prominent when his agent had left him. Was it coincidence that after his visits, her husband would come looking for her and take her to bed? .

Well today, she would be far away out of his sight. She was annoyed with his presumption that she should be there for him whenever he desired yet gave nothing of himself to her. Admittedly, she had promised him an heir and she knew that it was her duty to provide him with one. Surely though, there could be certain times when she need not be there for him when the mood suited him.

Often, she felt used by him. A tool; something in which he could assuage his desires if and when he required!

Hey Arabella, come here I have need of you to make me feel better!

She imagined him thinking along those lines and smiled at her own childishness. Her smile faded when she realised that she never could make him feel better. In fact she appeared to make matters worse. That was the problem!

He always gave her the utmost pleasure, if she was honest with herself, but they didn't conversed about anything important. It was as though he refused to allow himself to become better acquainted with her mind. Truth to tell, she was lonely. At that moment, she decided to become more herself in their relationship and vowed she would not accept his poor treatment of her. She needed to feel valued and she could not fulfil that desire unless she changed her tactics a little. She refused to become her mother.

Strolling around the garden during the morning sunshine eased her feelings of resentment. Castigating herself for becoming maudlin, she allowed the peace and quiet to sweep over her and renew her spirits. A brisk walk would blow the cobwebs away. Arabella surveyed the grounds. She could see a lake in the distance and made a mental note to visit it soon and then turning towards the side of the old property she noticed a small wood not far away. Delighted with her discovery she decided to stroll towards it. It was just what she needed to regain her normally calm, composed demeanour.

****

Meanwhile, Sebastian was feeling restless and hemmed in while he slouched back in his chestnut, leather chair in his study. He longed for a brisk gallop on Devil, his black stallion. Maybe he would ask Darcy to accompany him on a ride and even ask Arabella along. Did she ride? He hadn't thought to ask her.

In fact, there was very little he knew about the woman that could shake his very foundations and give him so much pleasure. In those moments of passion, he often felt she had consumed him, body and soul.

God help him, he didn't know what to do, anymore. He found it difficult to concentrate on anything and looked forward to the nights he spent exhausting himself within her. He felt so vulnerable and knew she had the power to destroy him. Funny thing was, she was unaware of that power. Gradually, his thoughts returned to state business.

Banks, his steward had nothing to report that he did not already know. Most of his estates were thriving, turning a huge profit. There were a couple small properties in Yorkshire that were steadily losing money and they had done so for the last few years but harsh weather conditions were much to blame for that.

Even in his father's day, they had proved to run at a loss. On the whole, his finances were in excellent health.

His thoughts returned to his heir. "Did you check on Rutherford's financial situation like I asked?"

Banks pulled out a folder and passed it to him. After surveying it for a few minutes, he sighed and threw it across the desk in frustration.

"I was sure he would be lying, but this confirms quite categorically all that Rutherford has told me. His wealth, his Shipping firm, his Estate! God, the man will equal my finances if he continues with his investments. I would say these were very impressive figures. He has definitely been busy."

"Indeed he has, your Grace. Turned over a new leaf as it were if you don't mind me saying so." Banks looked uncomfortable for a moment but continued,

"He gives the impression of being somewhat of a loose screw yet his business sense is admirable and he has recently excelled at estate management. Yet to hear the gossips, well……. You would think him a rake of the first order."

"I agree and can honestly say he has surprised me.

After concluding his business with Banks, Colby entered but again had nothing tangible to report.

"Have you had the men doubled on the estate?"

Colby nodded, "All's very quiet though, your Grace. Nobody has seen anything untoward."

"Keep an extra watch on the duchess at all times." He ordered, worrying about her safety.

"If it is Rutherford, then she is in as much danger as I am." He mused.

Yet somehow, he was beginning to think that his cousin was totally innocent and more than likely a victim in the same way as himself. The problem was if not Darcy, then who else could gain from his demise?

"Very well, your Grace." Colby answered, "Consider it done. I have placed someone in the house as a footman and another as a stable hand outside. Harris and Simms respectively. They're both men well used to ferreting out information, as it were."

With that, Colby left the room leaving Sebastian with a great deal to think about. Darcy he reluctantly agreed was unlikely to be after the title. Thinking back to when they were young men together, he remembered the happy go lucky youngster that stood beside Andrew and himself; laughing and joking about everything. There had been no ounce of guile in him. Yet, he could not afford to let him off the hook as yet. His wife's and his own life were in danger and it was too dangerous to trust anyone.

The report that Dulcie had been with a tall, blonde stranger who those present that fateful day assumed was Darcy had destroyed their friendship. Maybe he had been wrong all along. Perhaps Darcy was innocent.

But if not him, then who the hell was with her prior to the accident or murder?

After his third brandy, a habit he was beginning to recognise as a frequent occurrence lately, his thoughts turned again to Arabella.

At present, she appeared to be busy within the house implementing plans to redecorate the rooms. He was grateful for the changes taking place around him as the garish colours jarred on his already stretched nerves.

He had sent Darcy off to complete the signing of some documents with his steward while he talked to Colby. Now he was free to contemplate his wife. Sebastian comforted himself with the thought that he had the good sense to forbid Arabella to go unescorted outside, although he realised he had been heavy handed in his manner. Although guilt warred within him, he had to protect her in case there was a killer out there.

Despite everything he had been told, he still did not completely trust his heir and unless they could discover another tall, blonde gentleman, then Darcy would remain within the frame. As much as he did not wish it to be so, he could not see who else it could be.

His thoughts turned to Arabella once more and he felt the familiar hardening in his groin. He wanted her. How it scared him. She had become his obsession and he had used her continually to assuage his passion. He knew it was unfair.

He should treat her with respect! He owed her that much. His only excuse for his deplorable behaviour towards her was that he was trying his best to remove these feelings that consumed him. Trouble was, nothing he did worked, however many times he took her to bed. He was ashamed of himself for treating her no better than a common trollope.

Thoughts veered towards this morning when he had visited her. Each time he took her she was so generous in giving herself to him. It made him feel humbled, especially how he treated her afterwards, leaving before he could say something stupid like he loved her. God forbid. He needed none of that nonsense at the moment. Didn't he have enough to contend with?

For once, in a very long time he was ashamed of his behaviour. She did not deserve such treatment from him. He must open up in the same way as had. The thought of enjoying a complete relationship with her filled him with wonder, but he still felt nervous when he considered the possibility. There was always that danger of betrayal lurking in the back of his mind; of becoming a laughing stock once again.

Yet when he thought about it objectively, he could not imagine Arabella cheating the way Dulcie had. She was different. Arabella was a lady in every sense of the word. He sensed she was honest even though he had believed otherwise in the beginning. How quickly his opinion of her had changed. Ironically, the dark, haired Arabella was the light that brightened up his life while the blonde, haired Dulcie had been the darkness that invaded his soul.

He frowned at the way he had expected Arabella to do his bidding, making her a prisoner in her own home. If anyone had tried to dictate to him in a similar fashion, he would have disobeyed them. This afternoon he would make up for it. He would take her for a drive across the estate and perhaps have a picnic.

Yes, she would like that. In fact, he would do it now. No time like the present! Striding to the hall, Sebastian called for Danvers. Instantly, the butler arrived.

"Ah, Danvers, have you seen my wife?"

"Yes your Grace," he replied, woodenly, "her Grace went for a walk in the grounds about an hour ago. To my knowledge, she has not yet returned."

"And who did she have in attendance?" Sebastian asked, a knot forming in his stomach.

Danvers looked perplexed. "Her Grace left on her own."

"Arrange a search of the Hall and the grounds , immediately," he barked, fearing the worst.

"Very good, your Grace." Soon, Sebastian could hear Danvers calling the household staff together. He went to the library and fetched a pistol out of the cabinet.

Better to be armed in case of trouble, he thought.

Peering through a window he noticed that dark clouds had formed. He called for Molly and asked if she knew if his wife had worn a warm cloak.

"I do not believe she has, your Grace." She carried a blue cape over her arm in case Arabella had strolled out without one.

"At least she did not return to her rooms before she went out. I do not think it was planned you see."

"Does she often take a fancy to go out without a cloak?" he asked, exasperated by the trouble women brought to his life and secretly panicking at the thought of what could happen to her by herself out there.

"Not in town, your Grace, but I expect she didn't plan to go far. I have taken the liberty of fetching a warm cape in case she is still outside."

"Good, give it to me." He snapped, becoming more agitated by the minute. We will see if we can discover her whereabouts."

Just at that moment, there was a sound of carriage wheels coming to an abrupt stop outside.

"Who the devil is that?" he snarled, as he was greeted with the hustle and bustle and noise of a person descending on his home. "Good God, and who are you, Sir?"

The middle aged man bowed low and with a beaming smile said,

"Reverend Jonas Althrop at your service, Your Grace, come to see the new duchess. We have a great deal of business to discuss about the orphanage."

Much put out but with no time to see to this unexpected guest now, he turned to Mrs Hobbs and asked her to prepare a room for the reverend.

"Make yourself comfortable, but you will have to excuse me for a while. Urgent business"

He turned to ensure that his previous orders had been carried out and heaving an exasperated sigh, rushed outside to continue his search, leaving Althrop with his housekeeper.

The confused reverend looked askance as he heard the duke barking out orders to all his staff.

Strange fellow, he thought to himself as he followed Mrs Hobbs into the drawing room, somewhat mollified as he accepted a glass of the duke's best port.

Meanwhile, the duke was becoming frantic, wishing he had kept Arabella under lock and key for her own safety. For the next hour he searched but to no avail.

Where could she be?

He ran down to the lake, searching the boathouse and the surrounding area for any traces of her. He returned to the house to see if anyone had found her, but to no avail.

Surely, she would not venture into the woods?

He called for assistance in the unlikely case she had ventured up the crest to the woods. It was a good thirty minute walk and he doubted she would go so far on her own. Then again, did he really know her and what she liked to do?

Servants followed in his wake until he was almost there when suddenly a gunshot winged its way through the air. His insides somersaulted in an instant and he increased his pace as his imagination ran riot.

Maybe a poacher, but where are the men I hired to protect us?

He could hardly breathe, his throat so dry, his breath came in rasps. He ran as fast as he could until he reached the trees then plunged through the undergrowth searching all the time.

"Arabella," he shouted not caring who heard the panic in his voice.

Suddenly, he became aware of the sound of horses hooves and then into his line of vision came Darcy riding his stallion and leading his own stallion, Devil by the reins.

"I hear Arabella is missing," he stated, concern in his voice.

"I heard a shot and there is no answer when I call her name." Sebastian replied in a strangled voice.

"Have you tried the woodcutter's cottage?" Darcy asked.

In his panic, the duke had forgotten about the small cottage that nestled in the middle of the woods. He had not visited it for years. "No, not yet!"

"Then come," Darcy said, "hop on your horse!"

After giving his servants instructions to search and leave no area uncombed, he gratefully mounted his black stallion and followed Darcy through the thicket, all the time calling her name in the hope she would answer. They reached the clearing where lay the woodcutter's cottage to see a small boy engrossed with puppies , chasing them as they ran to and fro.

The rain had stopped and the sun was beginning to break through dull clouds when they dismounted.

"You, boy!" The duke shouted above the noise of the puppies who were barking as if in competition with one another, "have you seen a fine lady walking through the woodland?"

"Yep, I seen two fine ladies, Guv!" he replied. Darcy looked at Sebastian in confusion.

"Was one of them wearing a blue gown?" Darcy asked aware that Sebastian's mouth grew grim at his words.

"Well, when I greeted her in the dining room this morning she was wearing blue." Darcy explained, in an exasperated voice.

"I am surprised you noticed the colour of her gown!" Sebastian grated, annoyed that Darcy should remember when he had not. She always looked lovely in any colour.

"I," Darcy responded, "am not an old married man."

"Yep," the young boy haled, "That be the one whom sitting with me mum at the moment in there." Pointing to the door.

Both men rushed towards the open door of the cottage, and the duke gave a peremptory knock before barging through calling his wife's name.

"Sebastian," her melodious voice cried, "Is that you? Come into Mrs Bridges' parlour and see what she has been so kind to give me."

Relieved that his wife was unhurt he rushed into the parlour to discover her reclining with her foot on a stool and a puppy of dubious breeding, lying against her breast, wagging his tail and methodically licking her hand.

Mrs Bridges respectfully stood and curtseyed to her illustrious company who greeted her in turn.

"Only think, I was silly enough to turn my foot on a stray twig and Mr Bridges who heard my cry assisted me. He is now investigating poachers as we heard a gunshot."

"Which proves that it is not a safe place for the Duchess of Somerville to be wondering around on her own." The Duke admonished in a voice that threatened retribution.

"Nonsense, Sebastian, I was perfectly safe. Only see, I had my derringer with me."

To say that both gentlemen looked surprised was an understatement.

"Where, may I ask did you get that?" He rasped, shocked to the core.

"Can you use it?" They both asked one after the other.

"It was my father's and yes, I can use it very well. I am known to be fairly accurate at my mark."

"It would not stop a stray bullet, though." Her husband stated though secretly thrilled by the knowledge that his wife could shoot a gun.

"No, nothing would, your Grace, but you cannot live life worrying about stray bullets."

He was surprised that for once, there was an edge to his wife's voice that he had never heard before. He had obviously displeased her with his warning but what else could he do to protect her?

"So," he remarked, deciding to keep the conversation light, "Am I correct in understanding that we have acquired a new puppy?"

A smile lit her face, chasing away the previous frown. He realised that he disliked to see her annoyed and it was as though the sunshine appeared with her dimples.

"Oh, yes. Mrs Bridges says I may keep him if you are in agreement and I am sure you will come to love him as much as I already do."

She handed the puppy to him and he gingerly took the mongrel wondering what he had let himself in for.

"Jem has trained him so Molly may take him out when I am busy. You need not worry yourself over him. I daresay Mrs Hobbs will arrange his feeding time for me so you can have no real objection." She stated, looking up at him enquiringly, a challenge in her tone.

"I am sure you will have all the assistance you need with looking after him." Gently, he placed the puppy in her arms. His Grace's eyes were for once dancing as he surveyed the beautiful sight of his wife with this little puppy.

How will she look with my child in her arms?

He could not wait for that day to come.

Shortly, they took their leave of Mrs Bridges, the duke explaining that they had company at home and thanking her for her hospitality. He carefully picked up his wife and set her safely with the puppy on his stallion, swinging himself up behind them. Darcy followed on Gold Fire.

The duke would be glad to have her safely at home, protected from the outside horrors.

Thoughts still bothered him as he trotted home with his wife in his arms. Just who fired that shot and who was the other woman that Jem had mentioned?

Chapter Ten

Arabella reclined in the morning room with her injured foot elevated. Scamp, her little puppy, was taking the air with Molly so the room was quiet for once. For three, long days, the duke had insisted that she rest it until the swelling went away.

Arriving home that day, he had promptly arranged for the doctor to call, brow beating the elderly man mercilessly, to agree to order rest for the duchess. Arabella had challenged Sebastian, completely exasperated with all the fuss about such a minor injury. Unfortunately, he would not be gainsaid and so she reluctantly acquiesced to his wishes. She made a decision that in future he would not have his own way in everything. She believed it would not assist their relationship if he dictated her choices. After all, she was not a puppet.

For the first time since her outing, she sat on her own. It was early morning and the duke had carried her first to the dining room and then into the peaceful drawing room for a rest. He had only just excused himself, after ensuring her comfort, explaining that he had pressing business with Darcy.

She had missed his presence as he had not come near her bedroom to be with her since her slight accident.

Is he tiring of me? He appears to care for my well-being!

The thought made her feel uneasy! She had to admit that she enjoyed this attentive side to the duke, who showed such concern. So much so, that Arabella could easily convince herself that he cared just a little for her. She must pull herself together and remind herself that theirs was a marriage of convenience. He was still in love with his first wife. That was the only reason she could justify his anger every time they made love. He still left her bed and walked away afterwards as though he couldn't wait to leave her room. She truly believed that he felt disloyal to Dulcie! She would need to be patient with him.

With fondness she remembered their return to the house. After a minor scold for going out without advising anyone; he had offered her an apology for his crass behaviour since the day of their marriage. Arabella wondered what had brought about this volt-face, while at the same time, she had to admit that she liked the new, more humble side of the duke. At least this one was approachable.

Since that day, they had discussed the orphanage and many aspects of her life in Muchbury. He had appeared to be genuinely interested and for the first time in over four weeks, she felt relaxed in his company when they conversed. She was amazed that he should be interested in her life, but when he offered her assistance, she was gratified that at last she had someone who would possibly find the solution to the problem of the orphanage. He had promised to help her interview applicants for the position of Matron and also offered his services on the Board. She was incredibly grateful for his interest.

For after an interview with Reverend Althrop, she now knew where his interests lay. He had explained in detail, the whole matter to her.

Apparently, a week ago, Althrop, who had travelled to town to see Lady Arabella had decided to partake of his supper at his club and then pay a morning call the next day to apprise her of the progress of the orphanage.

"I did not then know you had married, your Grace," he admonished, secretly a little peeved at the absence of an invitation to the wedding.

After all, I have known her for years!

"It was a small affair," Arabella explained but then listened quietly to the shocking story.

On the first evening in town, he had entered into conversation with Sir Hilary Farthindale whom he had met by surprise at his club in London. Having spent the last five years hanging out for a rich wife, Farthindale had cast his net in the direction of none other than the Lady Henrietta.

"Unaware of Althrop's long standing passion for the lady, he had freely discussed his plans to net himself a fortune.

"You're a bit young for her, don't you think?" Althrop asked forthrightly, to which Arabella raised her eyebrows, but said nothing.

"My dear Althrop, all the better!" Farthindale smirked. "The conquest will be much easier. Admittedly, she is older, but not above ten years I would judge."

He took another sip of his drink, "I wonder I didn't find her before. She's worth a bit!"

Althrop had gritted his teeth and held his temper to prevent himself from giving the bounder a black eye. He would ensure that Lady Henrietta was fully apprised of the situation so that she could prevent herself from being taken in.

"And that is what I did, your Grace and how I came to visit you here. Lady Peabody advised me of your direction so I thought I would take it upon myself to come down immediately."

"But Althrop, I had no idea that you felt a grand passion for Lady Henrietta. Is it reciprocated?"

A smile played over his craggy features as he pondered the question.

"That, I do not know, your Grace. It was years ago, but I have grown older and she has grown richer. Even though my late wife bestowed upon me a considerable sum, dear Lady Henrietta may not countenance a match now. Her father thought me beneath her years ago."

All she would say to Althrop was, "You may be pleasantly surprised."

Now, returning to the present, she luxuriated in the peace and quiet of the morning room. Although she had been ordered to keep her ankle elevated, she could not see there was a real need to do so. It had healed and all the tenderness had disappeared.

She frowned.

Such a fuss about nothing! He is probably worried in case I am with child and fall down the stairs like Dulcie.

She was sure it was the only reason he was intent on confining her to the sofa for so long. Smiling secretly to herself, she allowed her hands to follow the contours of her flat stomach. How she would love to have the duke's child.

A knock roused her out of her reverie and a smiling Mrs Hobbs walked into the room and came to stand in front of her.

"Your Grace," she said retaining the smile, "how are you feeling?"

"Very well, Mrs Hobbs, very well indeed." Arabella gingerly stood on the aggrieved foot. Her face wreathed in a smile when there was not an ounce of pain and she slowly strolled back and forth a few steps to show the housekeeper how well she could walk.

"As you can see, I am right as a trivet. Now, how can I help you."

"It is the decorators, your Grace. Only fancy, they have discovered a secret panel in the Duchess Suite that they say, leads towards the end of the garden."

Arabella's eyes lit up.

"Oh, how exciting! Do you think his Grace knows about it?" She remembered just how old the Hall really was. "This house must date back to Cromwell's time so I wonder who they hid behind the panels."

"As to that, your Grace, I really wouldn't know. I do know that it has never been discussed as far as I can remember unless it was a family secret of course."

Mrs Hobbs followed her movements as Arabella strolled towards the window.

"Do be careful, your Grace."

"Nonsense, Mrs Hobbs, I am all healed, but tell me, where in the garden can we expect to materialise if we follow the passageway!"

Mrs Hobbs laughed. "As to that, I think they said that the opening was just passed the kitchen garden in the wild area at the back of the house. There is a walled garden there your Grace."

"A walled garden as well?" Arabella's almond eyes shone like stars.

"Yes, your Grace, though it's not been used for years. Her Grace took to sitting there when she was expecting the twins for a while but then seemed to lose interest and to my knowledge, it has remained unused ever since."

"But this is beyond anything. I wonder who has the key!"

The housekeeper smiled fondly. "Shall I persuade the gardeners' to prepare it for the summer months, your Grace?"

"Do you mean to say they have a key?" She became ecstatic at the prospect.

"I'm sure they have, your Grace. They would not leave it to a wilderness. Depend upon it. It will probably need a bit of sprucing up after the winter that is all."

Arabella could not believe how thrilled she was about a secret garden all to herself. Somewhere she could sit, she thought, and watch nature and gather her thoughts. It would be a quiet space where she could take her embroidery and bathe in the warm, summer sunshine.

She would hunt out the duke and advise him about the passage way.

"What do I tell the decorators, your Grace? Do you want the passageway blocked up?"

"I will talk to the duke and let you know the outcome as soon as possible. Thank you, Mrs Hobbs." Arabella hurriedly left the room, leaving her housekeeper smiling as she watched her mistress run towards the duke's study.

****

Meanwhile, the duke was in conversation with Darcy, Mr Bridges, the woodcutter, and the local magistrate.

"I hope you will understand the need to keep this information away from my wife, Sir Edgerton. I would not see her overset unnecessarily."

The magistrate pursed his lips and pondered upon the problem.

"If you are sure she did not see anything, then we need not risk upsetting her at this point, your Grace. I am sure we can discover the culprit but I would warn her of the wood's dangers at this time, if I were you."

"Of course. She will be accompanied wherever she goes." The duke replied, wondering what excuse he could set forth to ensure her hackles didn't rise. His wife, he was discovering was not quite as amenable as he had once thought.

"It may be best if you tell her that there are a band of poachers working in this area. That should keep her away." Sir Edgerton advised in a serious tone, concerned that the duke would not allow him to question the duchess. He would allow this for the time being, but at some point he would like to know if she saw anything suspicious. The duke appeared surprisingly over protective with his new wife.

"She would probably be more likely to try to rescue the puppies and Mr Bridges' son if I told her anything like that." Said the duke.

Both Mr Bridges and Darcy agreed laughingly, but then sobered as they were aware that a lady found dead in the woods was no laughing matter.

"Are you sure it was murder?" Darcy asked. "Could it have been an accident?"

"The shot was through the heart and at very close range. Whoever fired that gun pointed it at that woman and shot to kill, your Grace."

Sebastian was filled with horror.

Whoever it was could have believed the woman was my wife!

"You say she was dressed in fine clothes like that of a duchess," the duke queried, his stomach twisting into knots at the thought of his wife in such danger.

"Yes, much finer than my wife could afford." Sir Edgerton stated in a jocular tone. She could be someone from the aristocracy but she has the look of a street urchin, if you get my meaning."

"In what way do you mean?" the duke asked curious to know the line of thought Sir Edgerton might be pursuing.

"Well, her nails were full of grime and her hands were far more coarse than one would expect them to be. Her dark hair was also very dirty and you could not describe her in terms of refinement." Sir Edgerton stroked his grey whiskers, vividly remembering the unpleasant sight in the woods when he had been summoned to the scene of the crime.

Poor lass had been too young to die so tragically!

"So we are talking about a servant dressed in a rich person's clothes. Tell me, Sir Edgerton, could the killer have been mistaken, thinking that this person was my wife?" Cold shivers were running up his spine as he waited for the reply.

He didn't answer straight away. Sir Edgerton cleared his throat and looked uncomfortable then replied,

"I think there is a possibility that this person could have been mistaken for your wife, your Grace, but I don't wish to alarm you unnecessarily. Do you know of any person holding a grievance towards her?"

"Not at all. She has no enemies that I know of."

"Nevertheless, I would keep her away from open spaces until we can get to the bottom of this. We may be barking up the wrong tree of course, so don't start worrying just yet. After all, at this point, we don't even know the woman's name."

Numerous theories were discussed over a glass of port, until Mr Bridges and Sir Edgerton thought it time to take their leave.

"If you can think of anything further to add….." but Sir Edgerton did not finish his sentence because suddenly the door opened and like a burst of light, in rushed Arabella, her eyes shining, full of laughter, seemingly ready to burst with excitement.

"Oh Sebastian, you will never guess……oh, I am sorry I did not know you had company. Good day to you Mr Bridges and how is your wife and Jem and the puppies?"

"Very well, your Grace, thank you." Mr Bridges replied, laughing heartily. He thought the new duchess a breath of fresh air.

She turned to her husband and noticed his face was drawn in grim lines.

"Arabella, may I present Sir Edgerton who is the local magistrate."

She smiled, walking towards him with her hands held out graciously in a warm greeting.

"Good day to you, Sir. I hope this is a friendly visit." A slight frown appeared on her face.

"Yes, your Grace, I was in the neighbourhood so I thought I would pop in to enquire if his Grace new of any poachers in the district."

"Why yes, he does, because I told him about the one we heard while I was in the woodcutter's cottage a few days ago." Mr Bridges went in search of them, did you not?" looking at the woodcutter for authentication.

"That's right, your Grace, but I was unable to apprehend them."

"I'm sorry to hear it, Mr Bridges." Arabella said.

The duke turned towards Sir Edgerton,

"You will forgive us, Sir, but my wife and I have a previous engagement."

They showed their visitors out and then Arabella turned to the duke resuming her conversation without preamble.

"Did you know that there is a secret panel in the Duchess Suite that leads down to a garden?"

By the look on his face and that of Darcy's they were both unaware of it. She was elated thinking that they could share this adventure together.

"Why are you walking on that foot?" the duke asked, suddenly realising she was not resting on her couch where he had left her.

"Because it has healed. Please don't change the subject." Arabella warned, annoyed that he could dismiss her exciting find. She felt like stamping her foot in frustration. He appeared not to take her seriously.

The duke pulled out a chair for her and waited patiently until she sat down.

"Right, now tell us what you have discovered." He seated himself and gave her his full attention.

Arabella repeated what Mrs Hobbs had said and the duke and Darcy listened intently. She was surprised to see a certain gleam in Darcy's eye as she recounted the details.

"Well! It would seem our ancestors had their secrets." The duke drawled.

"But why the Duchess Suite?" Arabella asked, "I would have thought secret panels were more for the political intrigue of the time this house was built."

"It was not always the Duchess Suite." Sebastian explained. Only recently has it become so. Probably in my parents' time. My father obviously overlooked a secret panel."

Arabella wondered if the duke and duchess spent romantic evenings in the garden then dismissed the idea. They would have no need to hide in a garden. They could wonder freely over the estate. No, it must have been made purposely to hide people for political reasons. But surely, there was a possibility that when Dulcie had the rooms refurbished, she would have known about the secret panel. She made up her mind to peak in her diary to discover if she had indeed, been aware of it.

"I think we need to block the wall up, but I will have a look at it first. I cannot like the idea of free access to the Duchess Suite from the garden." Arabella and Darcy agreed.

Arabella had to reluctantly excuse herself when she heard Reverend Althrop's booming voice talking to Danvers.

"When is the fellow to leave?" asked Sebastian who did nothing to hide his impatience with the reverend whose sole topic of conversation appeared to be his Grace's hunters.

"He has advised me that Aunt Constance and Lady Henrietta are to pay us a visit in a couple of days so I have asked him to stay for another week. He is a great friend of Lady Henrietta, I believe."

Not by one muscle did his Grace show disapproval but Arabella perceived that he disliked the idea of more visitors at this moment. She was beginning to sense when the duke disliked a notion.

"You will not be vexed with entertaining them if you do not like it, your Grace, but I must own, I shall be glad of the company for a while."

"You will need to forgive me again, Arabella" the duke said, "put it down to my gross selfishness. Darcy and I are engrossed so often in business matters, I forget that you may feel isolated, somewhat."

"Excuse me for a moment, there is something I need to retrieve from the library." Darcy explained and left the room.

"Arabella, are you unhappy?"

"No your Grace, definitely not. I do like my aunt's company, however."

"The name is Sebastian, Arabella and you are welcome to your visitors if it makes you happy. You must forgive me if I am a little preoccupied at present. There is much on my mind lately."

Arabella moved close to him and placed her hand on his arm, a look of concern on her face.

"Forgive me for pestering you, Sebastian, I only thought to share the news of the panel. I did not think that you might have important business when I barged in just now." She glanced up into his chiselled features, sincerity plain to see on her face.

"I do know you are extremely busy and would hate to think that you felt you needed to amuse me. I am quite used to my own company, but would like it very much when our aunt visits."

The duke's expression softened as he looked tenderly into her clear dark eyes.

"I promise you, when this business which Darcy and I are engrossed in at present is over, I will take you away on a belated honeymoon and I will spend every hour of it in your company."

"I do not ask for your company, Sebastian. I do understand that you are extremely busy and I have plenty activities that I may happily pursue."

"Yes, I am sure you do, but I, on the other hand would like to know my wife a little better."

Arabella felt herself quiver inside as his eyes took on a smouldering look. She could not for the life of her break the contact and felt herself grow very warm as he moved closer and gently took her lips. The kiss was everything that she could hope for and left her wanting so much more. Somehow, she pulled herself together and put some distance between them.

"I must go, because I promised Jonas that we would discuss the orphanage today." Her voice was husky. "And Sebastian," she said pleadingly, "Please, do not have the secret panel blocked up until I have seen it!"

"Of course not!" the duke replied, "but I do not wish to hear that you have looked at it on your own. We don't yet know if it is safe and I think I would like to accompany you when you decide to explore."

She smiled at him, "Of course, but can we look at it today?" she asked, her wide eyes brimming with glorious anticipation.

He laughed. "Yes, we will go after luncheon." Arabella took her leave pleased that the duke had become so amenable. *I like this man when he shows his softer side!*

****

"You fool!" The tall, fair-haired man glared at the dirty, unkempt figure before him, for once not keeping his face hidden. "An imbecile, that's what you are!" He paced back and forth in the musty room in his brown, many caped greatcoat which covered him from his neck to below his knees. Anger emanated from every cell of his body.

"To kill the wrong woman! Only you could do such a thing as this."

Jenkins looked belligerent as the gentleman castigated him for his mistake. And that was what it was. From the outset he had hated the thought of shooting a fine noble lady, but the gentleman had promised a goodly sum if he could pop off three people that stood in his way. That sum would set him up for life and he wasn't going to be cheated out of it.

He could retire from all this and go live in the country somewhere. He had come to the conclusion that he was not cut out for a life of crime such as this. Petty thievery was fine but murdering women! Well that was another thing all together. After he finished this job, he would get out of the game.

"I'll get her next time she walks out, don't worry." Jenkins stated trying to calm the man down. He had known many flash coves but this one had a fiery temper and he didn't trust him much. "I needs me money!"

The gentleman's eyes bulged with temper, his face taking on a purple hue. "Don't even think that I will pay you for what you did! The woman you killed was working for me. She was on her way to fetch something of the utmost importance to me. You bungled it."

"But she sounded exactly like your description you gave me. If anyone is to blame it is you. I wasn't to know otherwise. Wearing finery you said, dark hair, you said, walking the grounds. Well she was, and I weren't to know the girl was working for you. She looked like a duchess, she did. You should 'ave told me you was sending a girl."

"Enough!" The gentleman said. "Don't look to get paid for the mistakes you have made. Now, I will have to go and retrieve the information I want and that will be risky."

"You ain't paid me nothing yet and I done loads of killing for you. You are no gentleman, mister!" Jenkins stated. Poor Jenkins. That was possibly the worst words he could have said to this particular man.

"And you have made the last mistake you will make for me," the gentleman said, while pulling a pistol out of the pocket of his greatcoat. Jenkins didn't have time to feel fear as the gentleman's bullet bored into his heart.

He walked over to the prone body. "You've had your payment." He spat down at him. "I'll deal with the rest."

For years he had waited so that the timing would be right. Now, because of Jenkins' bungling, they would be on their guard. He needed that diary, though. Thanks to Jenkins, he would now be forced to take a grave risk.

On the other hand, perhaps the new duchess would be present in the room. He could kill two birds with one stone. Or should he? He must not get sloppy or else they would be on to him.

He could afford to wait for his crowning glory, but not for the diary. It contained information that could see him swing.

****

Chapter Eleven

"*B*ut why can't we go down and have a look?"
Arabella stood in the Duchess Suite looking at the panel with Darcy and the duke.

"It is far too dangerous!" the duke replied after looking into the darkness behind the panel.

"We do not know how long ago it was used and we cannot tell how safe it is. I will have experts look at it from the garden, but we must block this hole up immediately. I cannot like access to the house from this quarter. Why, anyone could steal themselves in at the dead of night."

"True," Arabella said. "At least we will still have a private garden." She was truly disappointed by his words.

"Yes, but until I change the locks, I would rather you didn't venture out alone. We do not know who else knows this secret."

Arabella looked confused. "I don't understand," she said looking from one to the other. "Has something occurred to make you feel that there may have been an intruder?"

"Not as such, my dear, but I would rather err on the side of caution than have something untoward happen." His face had that grim look that she often noticed when he was deep in thought and believed that no-one was paying attention to him.

Of course! He is remembering all the tragedies that have happened in the past and will take no chances with anyone.

****

Much later, the two men were deep in conversation sharing a drink together in the duke's study. Sebastian passed Darcy his second brandy and helped himself. He strolled to his favourite chestnut chair near the fireplace, taking the decanter with him. Darcy took the seat opposite and reclined, crossing his legs comfortably.

They sat, neither speaking while the ormolu clock could be heard marking the seconds.

"Well, what do you think?" the duke asked Darcy after a long silence.

Darcy glanced towards Sebastian stirring himself from a deep reverie.

"I think you were correct in your supposition that the passageway has been used frequently and recently. The thin layer of dust speaks of a few weeks, not years."

"And Dulcie's maid, the duke queried, "Do you agree that it was probably her that was shot?"

"It seems very likely," Darcy answered. "This you know, could give us the answer to many questions."

"Such as?"

"Did someone use the passageway to enter Dulcie's bedroom on the day she died. Was she pushed or perhaps even drugged?"

"The truth is, we may never know what happened. If it was indeed her maid that died, we have no way of knowing anything she could have been hiding."

"Not necessarily," Darcy replied. "I think she may have been returning to retrieve something that could incriminate either herself or someone close to her."

The duke raised his eyebrows. Once again, silence reigned. Both men thought of different possibilities.

"What if…….No, never mind," the duke ventured. "Although…….."

Darcy raised his eyes intent on the duke's words. Nothing appeared to add up. Once again frustration set in.

"Do we know anything about this Briany?" Darcy asked, "Where she came from. Who she was?"

"All I know is Dulcie brought her with her like I suppose, Arabella has brought her own maid. I know Arabella has known Molly since she was a young girl because I had her checked out. I did not think to have Dulcie's maid checked as she appeared to think so highly of her."

"Have you had the rest of the staff checked out as well?"

"Only the ones who haven't been here for years. They all came with excellent references."

"Perhaps we should have a search of Dulcie's belongings. We might find something that perhaps Briany was looking for." Darcy suggested.

"A capital notion. Let's do so now. No time like the present." Both men made their way up to the attic where Dulcie's belongings were stored.

****

Something was brewing between her husband and Darcy Rutherford. She did not understand their relationship which had blossomed from nigh on hatred into something like bosom beaus. In fact, they appeared inseparable. They were up to something together and she could not tell what it was.

When she was with them, their conversation was formal, where they discussed the weather or the latest interest in newspapers which were delivered frequently. Yet when they thought she was busy with the housekeeper or some other mundane task, they could be found closeted together either in the library or in her husband's study, whispering or talking quietly.

As soon as she made her presence known, they would spring apart or cease the conversation and change the subject to some benign topic that she knew did not interest them in the slightest. Why did men need their secrets? She would get to the bottom of it sometime, she knew.

Thoughts of her husband made her ache for his touch. Had Dulcie felt the same intensity that Arabella did every time she thought of him? She wondered around her bedroom at a loss to know what to do. Jonas had gone down to the stables, a favourite haunt of his, so she had some free time to rest.

Her eyes strayed over to Dulcie's diary lying on her dressing table. Earlier, she had taken it out, wanting to discover if Dulcie had known about the passageway. It seemed so wrong to look at it but maybe she would discover more about her husband. Dulcie had known him far longer than she had. Perhaps she would not mind if Arabella read it. She would definitely understand him better if she knew a little of his relationship with his previous wife.

Having retrieved the diary, she made herself comfortable on the chaise longue and opened the book to the first page. The writing was somewhat untidy and there were many ink stains but she started to read:

How I hate this place where Seb insists I stay. I hate being pregnant. I feel so ugly. When I tell him I am bored he has the effrontery to advise me to go and visit the neighbours or send food to the sick. As if I care for them! I want to be in London!....

Arabella raised her eyebrows wondering just how any woman could feel so unhappy when she was expecting a child. Why would she wish to be in London when she could absorb the peace and quiet of Huxton Hall? She read a few more pages of the same ilk feeling that perhaps Dulcie had been a little spoiled.

But then, she had been so very beautiful! Arabella thought.

Who could blame her for a little petulance if she had been a spoiled beauty! Sebastian had probably been so besotted, he had given her everything until he decided she should retire to Huxton Hall while expecting the baby. In this, she would have agreed with her husband. Far better than racketing around town, paying endless morning calls and attending tedious parties. He would quite naturally be concerned about her. Arabella flicked through the pages, once more:

I have hit upon a grand plan. I have decided to refurbish Huxton Hall in hideous colours and invite my friends from London to see the result. It will be such fun. They will be so shocked! What a laugh! We will have a masquerade party. It is decided. Seb will be livid but it is his fault for treating me so. I hate it here. If I am not allowed to go to London then London shall come to me. I cannot wait! He will be so angry. Serves him right!

So, she had refurbished the entire house to spite him. Arabella had secretly wondered how anyone could like the garish colour scheme that Dulcie had apparently chosen. Oh God! I bet he had been angry!

She continued to read on through the pages, thoroughly intrigued by the spoiled beauty until something made her sit up straight:

Only think, what fun I can have now. I have discovered a secret panel in my bedroom and it leads to the garden. I will be able to have some fun and no-one will ever know! The refurbishment is almost finished. The servants are miserable but I have my Briany who I have told must stand no nonsense from them. She is a good friend to me and will keep the peasants downstairs in their places. How I hated this place. But now it is showing some promise…

She did know about the secret panel, but what does she mean? Arabella turned the pages until she found the night of the masquerade:

Well, what fun I will have tonight. Many of my friends are here and all are dressing up. I am about to bathe and prepare for the evening. I cannot contain myself! It has been so boring couped up in this hole. The place looks grotesque but unfortunately, Seb is not here to see it so. Stuffy Sessions! The House of Lords will always come before my fun! He will come though. He will definitely be here once he hears of tonight's shenanigans. How I will laugh in his face! He deserves it for treating me so beastly.

Arabella was stunned. Dulcie had not loved Sebastian. She had tried to ridicule him in front of London Society. How he must have felt she could not begin to understand. How sad. They could have waited in elation for the birth of their baby.

Instead, Dulcie had concentrated on shaming him within his own home. She had deliberately decorated it in terrible colours and then, hosted masquerades without his knowledge.

She read on, hopelessly obsessed with the diary now and in no way feeling shame about reading it:

I don't know him; have never seen him before which makes it all the more exciting, but he is muscular and magnificent. I took him to the garden through the passage way. Such fun. He made love to me. Oh, how good he was! I wanted him to stay there all night but he said he had to leave. He has promised to come again and I am already aching for his touch. I have given him a key so that he can come to me again, soon!

Oh God! Arabella could not understand how Dulcie could betray Sebastian. Somehow, while expecting a baby, every sordid detail seemed to be worse.

Who was this man? She had made love to a man she didn't even know. Arabella made herself take a few calming breaths! At this moment, she felt so angry! When she had calmed herself a little, she continued. She must keep control of her emotions.

I love his muscular thighs next to mine. I cannot get enough of him.. The house party is over and once again I am on my own. Seb is coming down at the weekend for two or three nights. I will have J beforehand. I will have him in my bed all night tonight. Perhaps at the weekend, we can slip behind the panelling and do it. What fun that will be. Especially if

Seb is there, lying in his Duke's bed. J has promised me he will come. Briany brought the note. I think I love J. I have never loved Seb, but he knows that. He is so stuffy. Only thinks of being a Duke with duties. I need a man in my bed, not a duty. J will come, I know. I feel insatiable with him. How I wish I didn't carry this child. It's not as though I know who the father is!

Arabella closed the book and replaced it in the drawer then lay down on her bed. She couldn't read anymore at the moment. She could not believe what the woman had been capable of. How evil! Her heart went out to her husband who had loved this woman so much. She wondered if he knew. She didn't think so. After all, he hadn't had the will to clear out the Duchess Suite.

It had stayed there a monument to the woman who had betrayed him in every sense of the word. All Arabella wanted to do now was hold him and love him. She felt such pity for the man who had experienced such betrayal. How could this woman have done such evil things?

****

He was kissing her awake. Slowly, she was aware that her husband was lying next to her tenderly kissing her and holding her. As she came to her full senses, her body hopelessly aroused, she remembered Dulcie's betrayal. How could she begin to heal the hurt that he had suffered at the hands of such an evil woman?

His strong hands were finding all her sensitive parts. She responded immediately, so hungry for him. She needed him desperately and would show him how much. He deserved to be loved and God, how she loved this man. She would think about that later, but for now she would make love to him whether he liked it or not.

His kisses were petal soft and then whispered over her full lips. She gently bit them sending him into a spiral of desire. He reciprocated, smiling into her mouth.

"I want you!" he whispered close to her ear.

"I want you too; all of you." She replied tracing her fingers down his tanned face. His breath caught then his hands found their way to her full breasts. She was aching for his touch. He caressed her through the thin material of her dress then growing impatient, attempted to release her neckline. While his fingers were working her buttons, she was again biting his lips, while tracing the contours of his pants. For once, he did not pull her hands away so feeling bold, she began to unbutton his shirt. Immediately he tensed but she continued licking and biting him, for once feeling in control of their lovemaking.

He allowed her to continue as if in surrender which made her feel more powerful. Moving slowly, she lay on top of him and kissed him thoroughly, discovering a boldness she had been unaware of any time before.

She managed to take off his shirt and between them they undressed. Next came his trousers and his unmentionables until he was lying naked in all his glory before her.

She traced her fingers down his body in awe of his beauty. *Was she dreaming?* She sat up and then perused the length of him, seeing his manhood for the first time. Her hands slid slowly towards it and she clasped it holding it, feeling it throb.

"Move your hand up and down, slowly." His breath came in gasps. She complied watching the effect she was having on him, her body moving in unison. She suddenly knew what she had to do. She would place herself on top of him and he could enter her.

The feeling was unbelievable; his manhood entering her from this position. She revelled in moving her hands over his bare chest. She bent and kissed and licked his nipples until they became prominent like her own. Needing to feel his mouth, she took his lips in a savage kiss that saw them moving together in a rhapsody. She continued to devour his lips with her own and pushed her tongue into his mouth. He was going to climax and so was she.

She could not stand anymore of the intensity yet it went on and she rode the waves, screaming out in release. Very soon, she heard him cry out and they both slowly came down from their powerful orgasms.

They lay together gasping for breath still with their bodies entwined and his manhood inside her. God forgive her she still felt she could ride it and moved slowly on his hot rod. For once, there was no anger or pulling away. Instead, he said,

"Give me a moment your Grace and I will be able to oblige you."

She found the courage to kiss him fully on his mouth. "Thank you," she replied in a whisper.

"No, thank you. I rather like this new, bold duchess I seem to have acquired." His hands roamed over her breasts and she felt him move inside her.

"I rather like this new duke I seem to have acquired, your Grace."

She kissed and bit him on the lips which found him once again driving into her. She accommodated him comfortably and this time he took control, showing her his mastery over her body. Very soon, she found herself climaxing again.

****

Arabella heard the knock on the door as she came slowly awake. Her husband was still inside her and had been so while they slept. She was thrilled that she held him so close.

"It's time to get ready for your bath my lady. Shall I come back in ten minutes or so?"

"Tell her to make it half hour," he whispered.

"Come back in half an hour, Molly," she said obediently, and resumed the exploration of her husband's lips.

Dinner that night was animated and the four people present appeared to be in good spirits. Sebastian let his glance slide to his wife who was dressed in a peach, silk gown that fitted her like a second skin. She was truly beautiful, he thought, and she was all his. He knew now that he loved her like he had loved no other woman and couldn't wait to spend the night with her. He would sleep with her tonight; all night, although he doubted they would derive much sleep. Sebastian smiled as he imagined what they would share in a very few hours.

The gentleman did not linger over their port and Althrop said he would take a turn around the garden, before retiring.

Darcy and the duke had just settled to a game of billiards when Danvers announced that Lord Edgerton had called. After he was shown in, he came straight to the point.

"The woman shot in the woods, your Grace has been identified as Miss Briany Walker, who used to be a maid in the late duchess's employ. I believe that she was turned off recently by your wife."

"That is correct, Sir Edgerton, but I am at a loss to understand what she was doing on our property when she was informed that she should not come near."

"That, is what I would like to ask your wife, your Grace."

"I can see no reason to involve my wife, Sir Edgerton." His Grace answered, somewhat abruptly.

"Nevertheless, your Grace, I need to speak with her."

The duke searched the other man's face wondering why he wished to speak to Arabella. He could not see the necessity, but reluctantly succumbed to the magistrate's demand.

"Come this way!" he ordered in his most authoritative tone, "although I do not see why you must upset her. It will not bring the woman back."

"I'm sorry, your Grace, but your wife may know something that would help me with my enquiries. She was, after all, in the woods at the time of the shooting."

"Yes, but she was in the woodcutter's cottage, in conversation with Mrs Bridges at the time."

"That, I do know, your Grace, though, she may have seen something before she visited Mrs Bridges."

They moved towards the drawing room where Arabella sat with an open book on her lap.

"Good evening, Sir Edgerton," she greeted pleasantly, "to what do we owe this pleasure?"

Sir Edgerton explained his business, noting how shocked Arabella was but thankful that she was willing to help in any way she could.

It could have been me, she thought as she remembered tramping through the woods.

"The only person I saw was Mr Bridges after I tripped and fell."

"Did you hear anything? Footsteps or voices? Please think back to the time when you were in the woods prior to your accident."

Arabella took time to consider Sir Edgerton's words. Had she heard or seen anything? She did not think she had.

"A rustle of trees, but that would be normal and then it started to rain and I could hear the heavy droplets on the leaves. I remember looking around for some cover. The birds were singing and I could hear the puppies barking but could not see them. I do not remember anything else except for tripping on an exposed root."

"So when you fell, did you cry out for help?" Sir Edgerton persisted.

"Yes, I remember crying out as I fell and then within a short time, Mr Bridges was there to help me."

"From which direction did he come?"

"From behind me, because he made me jump out of my skin. I did not hear his footsteps, you see."

"And when you were helped towards the woodcutter's cottage, which direction did he take?"

"Well really!" The duke barked, "Is this absolutely necessary?"

"I am attempting to establish from whence Mr Bridges came. It is important your Grace."

"Mr Bridges came from the woodcutter's cottage as we only walked back the way he had come and it was hardly any distance." Arabella exclaimed. "I was never more thankful in my life. My ankle hurt so very badly at first."

"Are you sure about this, your Grace?"

"Absolutely," she responded with conviction ringing in her voice.

"As it happens, we were only about a hundred yards from the cottage. It was hidden from view by the trees.

"And you cannot tell me anymore? You did not hear anything else?"

"I am sorry Sir Edgerton, there is nothing more to tell."

"Then I thank you your Grace for your assistance. If you should remember anything else, please send me a message as soon as possible."

A short while later, Sir Edgerton left promising to let them know if he discovered anything else of importance.

"I wonder why Briany was walking through the woods," Arabella asked. "To be sure, I know she did not have a young man to walk out with at the Hall, as all the servants seemed to fear her."

"I do not know," Sebastian answered. "Perhaps she had forgotten something and was on her way back to collect it."

Arabella thought of the diary but did not wish to tell Sebastian about it. It would hurt him unbearably. She could not be the person who exposed Dulcie. It would seem like tittle tattle.

Better he retain fond memories.

Suddenly, Briany's words came back to her and she shivered involuntarily.

"You and your like will rue the day you dared to get rid of me!" The maid had stated, *"I knows things that will destroy you and his nibs. Just wait and see!"*

Just what did the maid mean by those words? At the time, Arabella thought she was merely being spiteful and vengeful, but now, after seeing the diary, she wondered if there was anything else in there that could throw light on her words.

She would plead a headache and go to bed. There, on her own, she would read the rest of the diary and try to discover if it was merely a need for plain vengeance or if there was something more that she needed to know to protect Sebastian.

Was that disappointment she saw on his face as she bade them both goodnight?

Chapter Twelve

She had taken three steps up the wide staircase when she heard a commotion coming from outside. Arabella paused and turned in anticipation as Danvers threw open the great double doors.

A familiar voice was heard that forced a smile upon her face. She hurried to the front door to greet her aunt and

Lady Henrietta, the former, giving orders to the footmen and maids who had accompanied them from London.

"Oh Aunt Constance, I did not expect to see you this evening."

"I apologise to you child for descending upon you at this late hour," she said as she hugged her warmly, "I felt it incumbent to bring Hettie away from London before she succumbed to silly ideas. You know what a scatter brain she is and Farthingdale is just too smooth in his addresses. I would hate to see the widgeon unhappy."

"But surely, she would not submit to Farthingdale's charm?" Arabella asked, shocked to think that Hettie could be so fickle.

"No my dear, but I do not leave anything to chance."

With that, Arabella gave instructions to Danvers and Mrs Hobbs who had suddenly materialised from the depths of the Hall.

She knew that her servants would ensure the comfort of her guests and could leave them to arrange everything to a nicety.

"Come into the drawing room, Aunt. Sebastian and Darcy are still there and will be pleased to see you. You too, Hettie. You will be pleased to know that Reverend

Althrop is to stay for a while longer. I hear you are acquainted?"

Hettie, who had entered the Hall after overseeing Lady Peabody's orders, blushed becomingly at the news of Althrop's presence.

"We do indeed know one another. In fact we knew each other very well when we were very young." She explained.

Presently, they were all comfortable in the drawing room having ordered tea and a light snack which both ladies thought was all they required before they would each retire to their rooms.

Once again, Arabella bade Sebastian and Darcy good night as she accompanied her guests to their rooms, ordered herself a hot chocolate to be brought up and retired to read the diary.

Molly was present waiting to prepare her mistress for bed and once she had brushed Arabella's hair the requisite hundred strokes and wished her a pleasant night's repose, she let herself out of the room.

As soon as she was ensconced in her comfortable bed lying back on the duck down, feather pillows, she once again opened the diary.

Much of it was the same as she turned the pages. Dulcie discussed the gentleman in detail, or rather her exploits with him, sounding like a young girl in the throes of a grand passion. She turned the pages as she read, disgusted and saddened by the woman who held Sebastian's heart.

How could she do this to him? She thought becoming more appalled as she read the words. Then suddenly, the tone of Dulcie's writing seemed to change. Arabella sat up as she read on. She was becoming bored with this person and peevish.

How common he is! I was sure at first that he was a gentleman with a wife and brats at home, but no! Instead, I discover a man with ambitions far beyond his station! I feel quite used by this man who thinks he can become duke! Preposterous barbarian! He would never measure up to Sebastian in gentlemanly behaviour. Perhaps that's what I liked about him. He is beginning to bore me now though with all his talk about the direct line. As if a man such as he could ever become duke! A commoner, no less and a bastard to boot!

Arabella put the diary down to try and understand what Dulcie had written. What did she mean or what, in fact, did this man whose name was beginning with 'J' mean? He could not be the heir because Darcy was. Unless there was something that no-one else knew. She read on a few pages, but these mainly consisted of Dulcie's complaints about the staff and Huxton Hall.

Apparently, she had become bored with this man and was looking for someone else to fill his shoes. It appeared that one of the footman had taken her fancy and she was planning to seduce him. As she read further pages, Arabella was horrified to discover that she had enjoyed a fleeting liaison with one of the gardeners and had actually seduced him in the walled in garden. Feeling frustrated and angry that she was unable to give the woman a piece of her mind, she was about to close the diary when her eyes fell on a passage that somehow beckoned to her. The last entry that Dulcie ever wrote:

Only think, he dared to threaten me! Me, a duchess! I told him to go and warned him that I would call the footmen, but he laughed and caught me by the throat. I do not like this man, he is evil. I fear for both Seb's and Darcy's life. He aims to kill them! That was what he told me and he said that he would take their place and I would become his duchess. As if I would marry a murderer! He is quite mad, I think! I would rather stay with Seb with all his boring ways. I must tell Seb when he comes tomorrow. I must warn him about the danger he faces. This man is capable of anything. Until then, I will pretend to agree with him. I must warn Briany as well as she has shown a decided interest in him recently.

Arabella's thoughts were reeling. Sebastian had been in danger from this man and so was his heir. Who on earth was he? She now knew what she must do. She must show Sebastian the diary. He could still be in danger from this man. She hoped they had sealed off the panel because else, he could still enter the Hall.

After everything she had read, sleep was impossible. She would need to go and see Sebastian now. Taking the diary, she gathered her wrap and descended the staircase. No doubt he would still be playing billiards with Darcy. Finding Danvers, she asked him where the duke was and was advised that he was in his study.

"Lord Rutherford retired a few minutes ago, your Grace and his Grace asked for his brandy to be brought to his study." Danvers voice was always so conciliatory and he was such a pleasant fellow.

"Thank you, Danvers, I need to speak to him."

"I will just announce you, your Grace."

"No need, Danvers, I will just enter as I always do!" she could see no point in the stiff protocol the servants always employed, often slipping past them before they had a chance to announce her.

"As you wish, your Grace!" and Danvers bowed and returned to the seat by the great double doors. It was his usual resting place at this time of the day, prior to retiring for the night.

Sebastian was sitting in the chestnut chair near the fireplace a glass of brandy in his hand. He looked up when she entered, a smile spreading over his face.

"This is a pleasant surprise. Has your headache gone, my dear?"

"Yes, it has quite disappeared, but I need to speak with you on a matter of urgency and I am afraid you are going to be angry with me."

A frown marred the perfection of his face.

"This, my dear, sounds ominous! What could you have possibly done in the short time you have been upstairs to cause me to be angry."

"It is not only tonight, Sebastian," she said in a small voice, trembling at the thought he would hold her in disgust at taking Dulcie's diary.

"Molly and I discovered something in the Duchess Suite a few weeks ago and until yesterday, when we discovered the secret panel, I had not thought much about it."

Sebastian's eyes never left her face as a look of shame washed over it. How he loved hearing that melodious voice. So very soothing. Just what had she been doing to make her feel so nervous?

"I think you better begin at the beginning my love, and tell me everything. Sit down and I will pour you a drink."

The endearment came quite natural to him until he saw a look of horror pass over his wife's features, quickly masked.

She sat down gracefully, aware of the endearment which at first warmed her until she realised that she was about to disappoint him more than he could ever believe.

Oh my dear love. You do not realise what I have done!

"I know I should have brought it to you right away, but I thought I could discover if Dulcie knew about the secret panel and then, after starting to read it, I could not put it down." She could not bear to face him and kept her eyes cast down as he placed the drink in her hands. She swallowed a large amount of the fiery liquid and spluttered and coughed.

"Sip it slowly and it will warm you. It is not a drink one should hurry especially when you are not used to it." He warned, smiling at her.

When she had recovered herself, she continued with her confession.

"I am so sorry, Sebastian, but I have read Dulcie's diary and I know you will be angry with me, but I think you need to read it as your life may be in great danger. In fact, you must believe me when I tell you that your cousin's life may also be in danger. You must be extremely careful. Oh, you are so very angry with me……………. Please forgive me."

Sebastian remained silent, staring at her, unable to speak; not knowing what to say. Once again, he had been given something without effort. He had failed to discover it himself. His wife had found the answers that he had sought for months. Was he always to be offered everything on a plate?

Yes, you are correct! I am angry, but not with you. With myself.

The answers had been there in the Duchess Suite and he had never bothered to enter. He had revelled in his own self-pity at his wife's betrayal and while he was doing so, people's lives had been in danger. He had failed them.

He reached for the diary and stared at it.

"You will not like what you read, I fear, Sebastian. I wish I could spare you from this heartache but I would wish you to take the threat seriously."

"Thank you, Arabella. Please believe me I am not angry with you for this. I am grateful that you have discovered something that may provide me with answers I have been seeking for the last few months." He reached out and stroking her hair, kissed her gently. "Go to bed, Arabella. I will see you in the morning."

"You are truly not angry with me?" She saw the truth in his eyes as he gazed at her tenderly.

"Good night, Sebastian," she said and quietly left the room, knowing that she was leaving him with words that would hurt him beyond belief.

****

The next morning, Sebastian was discussing the diary with Darcy. Contrary to Arabella's belief, the duke had not felt the least shocked at Dulcie's betrayal. He knew that she had been unfaithful from early on in their marriage.

What he was shocked by, was the knowledge that a fair haired gentleman had made himself at home in his first wife's bed right under his nose.

"It is someone whose name begins with 'J' but we don't know if Dulcie knew it. Does it ring any bells with you because it certainly doesn't with me."

"Oh come on, cuz, I know many people with the initial J. We both know James and have done so for years but he is neither tall nor fair haired so we can't pin it on him."

"It is like looking for a needle in a haystack." The duke stated, frustrated by the lack of knowledge.

"I know," Darcy replied, "but if we send a messenger up to London, I think we may discover who he is. Your lawyer may know something."

"Yes," the duke agreed, pensively, " I think he must have a connection somewhere with us, even if it is remote."

"Possibly, someone who resembles me a little. Enough so that I could be blamed for being with her the day she died." He said, ruefully, "Do you think he killed her?"

"As to that, it would appear so, especially if she was fool enough to let him know she would apprise me of the situation. It is the type of thoughtless act Dulcie was capable of. She invariable acted before she had thought things through."

Both men pondered upon the enigma of Dulcie. She had allowed a perfect stranger into the Hall, who could have stolen priceless artefacts and murdered people in their beds all because she was bored. Now, lives were in danger and something had to be done at once.

"I think Colby's footman Harris, can keep watch from now on by the panel. If he is after the diary, which I am now sure he is, he will surely enter through there." I must protect my wife at all costs.

"I think we need more than one footman to ensure the safety of the ladies. I don't think we should underestimate our man." Darcy warned, echoing his thoughts.

"Simms is another one of Colby's men presently working in the stables and looking out for anyone sinister. I could move him to the Duchess Suite and see if Colby can bring the other hired men closer to home. At the moment they are patrolling the boundaries, but the estate is too large for them to protect every area."

Darcy took another swig of his brandy and placed it down on the side table. For once the smile had vanished from his startling blue eyes and there was a look of exasperation on his face.

"I think this man will wish to seize the diary fairly quickly. He must be worrying about its content by now."

"I agree! We will all need to be vigilant, but I do not think we should underestimate him as if we are correct in our assumptions. The man could be a ruthless killer and if so, everyone under this roof may be in danger from him."

"So bring in more men!" Darcy stated.

"Yes, but I do not want the ladies to get wind of this. It is bad enough that Arabella has read about him. I do not want her worrying unduly."

"Better that she is on her guard, cuz!"

"Once again, you are correct! Better to be safe than sorry. I will have Colby organise the men immediately."

****

Aunt Constance was taking a tour of the Hall with Arabella commenting on the plans that she had implemented to date. The place was beginning to look decidedly fresh and they both loved the pastille colours that seemed to lift the rooms and make them so much brighter and elegant.

"Dulcie had deplorable taste!" Aunt Constance frowned, then glancing towards Arabella a warm smile creased her bony features.

"Sebastian must be able to see a tremendous difference. I know I can in only five weeks. You have done well, Arabella, just as I thought."

This was indeed high praise from Lady Peabody. She invariably gave her opinion on all things but more than often found something to grumble about. Arabella smiled, laughing at Scamp, who trotted merrily along by her side pausing every so often to sniff at the skirting boards.

"I am pleased that you like it. Tell me Aunt Constance, what is to happen between Althrop and Lady Henrietta? Will they make a match do you think?"

"I am sure they will, eventually, but I have advised Hetty to wait a while before she gives him an answer. It will stand her in good stead if she doesn't fall into his lap like a ripe plumb, as it were."

"And do you think she will take your advice?"

Lady Peabody raised her fine eyebrows, "But of course dear. She has always taken my advice."

Arabella wondered if Hetty would be so keen to take her aunt's advice now that Reverend Althrop had returned to her life after all these years. They strolled along the gallery which had not been touched examining the fine works of art and the portraits of Sebastian's ancestors. They looked to be all imposing men and women and Arabella felt humbled that she had been invited into such a magnificent family. Lady Peabody paused at a portrait of Sebastian's parents holding the twins. They all looked incredibly happy.

She glanced at her aunt who had a look of pride on her face, then back to the portrait. It was so tragic, to have their lives cut short. They moved on to a portrait of a young man who was the image of Sebastian. The young gentleman looked down on them with a smile upon his face.

"That was Andrew, Sebastian's twin brother. They were devoted to each other. It almost destroyed Sebastian when his brother died so tragically. He blamed himself you see. Of course he had nothing to do with the accident, but Sebastian is always prepared to take responsibility for everything that goes wrong in his life. I wish he would be kinder to himself."

"What a tragedy," Arabella stated, "I would have liked to have known him. You cannot mistake that they were twins. So much alike! Andrew looks to have had the Winslow twinkle in his eye. It appears to run through the family on the male line."

"Yes, a fine young man, poised for the dukedom. Sebastian was never interested, you know. Not until his brother died. Then when his parents perished, he made a promise to himself to do his duty no matter what the cost was to himself. He has kept that promise to this day."

"Yes, he makes a very fine duke." Arabella said with pride.

"And you, my dear, will make a very fine duchess by his side." Lady Peabody smiled at her god daughter warmly, giving her a hug.

"I really hope so, Aunt. I will promise to do my best."

If only he loved me as I now realise, I love him. What a future we could create together!

Turning towards the dear lady by her side, she said in earnest, "Please believe me Aunt I will try to make him happy."

"I know you will, child. "

They strolled further down the gallery and paused in front of a portrait of three men who were obviously brothers. The likeness was uncanny.

"We have here Sebastian's father Carlton, who married my sister and his two brothers. The middle one was Frederick who is Darcy's father and then there is Arnold on the right. It is sad that all three are dead now.

As you know, Carlton died in a carriage accident with my dear sister but Frederick died of the influenza. He always had a weak chest and died before Darcy was out of leading strings. Arnold was in the Army and met his death in the battle of Aboukir in 1801. He was led by Sir Ralph Abernathy. They defeated the French Army of Egypt but poor Arnold was slain. A very brave soldier!"

Lady Peabody had given her much to think about and when they retired to rest in their respective rooms before dinner, Arabella lay on her chaise longue facing the window with its magnificent view before her. She had meant every word she had said to Aunt Constance and knew she would strive to be a good duchess and an exemplary wife. With all the sadness in his life, her husband deserved some happiness.

His face, she noticed often looked grim until he became aware that she was watching him, then he would mask the worries he appeared to be dealing with. How she wished that he would share them with her.

She wished not only to support him in all his work but also his troubles. He shouldered his responsibilities alone and Arabella did not think that was necessarily the correct approach.

She cast her mind back to the previous evening at dinner. She had smiled and he had returned the smile until his eyes changed from a soft caress to a smouldering look that burned her skin. She remembered looking away in confusion. His passion could reach across the table and scorch her with its strength. Now, his life was in danger and she would do everything in her power to protect him.. Her derringer was safely tucked away in a pocket in the folds of her skirt. She would carry it always to ensure his safety.

Dinner that night was a pleasure as everyone gathered together. There was much talk of Farthindale and the like who appeared to haunt town in the hopes of a rich wife.

Lady Peabody related many tales of such matches where men married merely for a fortune and how the couples married in haste and repented at leisure.

Although the present company were unaware of his reason for marrying Lady Peters, Althrop seemed to cringe in his chair. His late wife's attraction had solely been the fortune she would bring him on their wedding day. It was true they had rubbed along together admirably, but his conscience, that on rare occasions reared its ugly head, was niggling uncomfortably at this precise moment.

"For I always say, if a man hasn't been used to a fortune, often he will allow it to slip through his fingers in an instant. Too many marriages based on fortunes have ended up with each hating the other and eventual poverty owing to the fact that the men tended to spend far too many nights at the gaming tables."

"I am sure you are right, Aunt." The duke replied. "Hettie must think herself exceedingly lucky to have you to guide her." Althrop spent an inordinate amount of time studying his fork.

"Oh yes," said Lady Henrietta, "I am conscious of the kindness my dear Lady Peabody shows to me."

"You need not stand on ceremony, minx! Call me Constance as you would normally. I am sure Althrop will be around for a long time so he may do so also."

Hettie was ecstatic with her words and look to the Reverend Althrop who was all smiles and gratitude, knowing the honour that Lady Peabody bestowed upon him. She blushed amiably and fluttered her eyebrows at her beau. If Constance approved of Jonas, all would be well. Not many were on first term names with the stern old lady and he was exceedingly pleased and beamed amiably at everyone for the rest of the evening.

He was even more grateful to be included in a game of cards when Arabella, Hettie and Lady Peabody decided to play after dinner. Even losing, did nothing to destroy his sense of pride.

Later, when it was time to retire for the night, he swaggered to his room feeling at least two inches taller and even more puffed up in his own consequence.

Chapter Thirteen

$\mathcal{S}$ebastian held Arabella close, his fingers tracing the outline of her swollen mouth that even now he couldn't resist kissing ever so gently not to disturb her. They had made love and he was still wanting this woman more than any other. He looked into her peaceful face as she slept.

Hers was a gentle beauty, not in the same way as Dulcie's. It was honest and pure and her personality shone from her eyes. Eyes that were clear and candid. He loved to watch her in all her moods, whether deliriously happy or pensive. There were other facets of her personality that he adored. She was innately good with people. Very natural, needing no artifice. Her voice was the most melodious he had ever known and he loved listening to her when she was conversing with either himself or others.

He remembered watching her play with Scamp in the drawing room. Previously, he had told her that this room was out of bounds to the puppy, but she had over-ruled him on this. If she disagreed with him, she would state her case and invariably, he was finding little reason not to give in to her. He smiled to himself.

That is what one does when one is in love!

He would not tell her yet. Not until he was sure she felt the same and so far, she had shown only that she accommodated him in the bedroom.
He knew she was physically attracted to him and that went a long way, but outside of love-making, she held herself back from him. It was as though there was a wall between them that he could not breach.

Of course, theirs' had been a marriage of convenience and he had told her to expect nothing else. But love had crept up on him. He had not looked for it. Now it was here, he was filled with a joy so complete, he wanted to hold her for eternity and protect her from everything that might cause her harm or discomfort.

He wanted and needed her love. He wanted her body, mind and soul and he would accept nothing less than her complete capitulation in all three. This would be worth waiting for and earning. He had patience. He would use it.

Sebastian must have slept, but he was awakened by a sound. Gingerly, he removed his arm from his wife's shoulders and went to investigate.

As he gently shut Arabella's bedroom door, he quietly summoned a waiting lackey who was posted nearby for her safety and ordered him to stay by the door until he returned. Nothing must disturb her sleep. Only he would have that privilege. The noises came from the west wing where Lady Peabody slept, close to the Duchess Suite. He strode towards the commotion and paused as he noted footmen and maids huddled around a prone figure.

"Stand aside," he ordered only to discover his aunt, lying deathly still on the floor.

"Summon the doctor immediately," he barked, "can anyone tell me what has happened here?"

"She said it was Lord Rutherford she saw, but he has run off now, your Grace. A maid answered in a timid voice.

"Harris came out of the Duchess Suite and gave chase, but no-one has seen him since."

"Are you sure it was him?" the duke asked, not believing it for a minute.

"Ohhh!" Lady Peabody groaned, "Help me up, I need to see Sebastian."

"I'm here, Aunt Constance, what happened?"

As Lady Peabody began to recover, she slowly sat up, still feeling groggy, and feeling the back of her head.

"The fiend hit me over the head and I saw stars." She explained, "I heard a noise outside my room, a scuffle of sorts and went to investigate."

"Who was it?" he asked quietly.

"Why it was Darcy! He was struggling with a footman of all things. I asked them what they meant by waking decent people up at this time of night and Darcy broke free of the footman, ran towards me and clocked me over the head with something that looked like a gun. I was never so shocked in my life, I can tell you."

"Are you sure you could see clearly in the dark, Aunt?"

Lady Peabody touched her head gently feeling around the injured part.

"I am not in my dotage yet, Sebastian…….. Look here, I have a lump, the bounder!"

"Aunt Constance, what made you think it was Darcy? In this light, it would be hard to tell, surely?"

His aunt looked at him in shock and disgust.

"Trust me, I am not going senile , Sebastian. I know what I saw and it was Darcy who ran up to me. Tall, fair hair! Nobody answers that description in this house except for him." The duke's blood ran cold.

"We will settle you back in bed and then I will go and see him. The doctor will be here to see you soon. Would you like me to call someone? Hettie or Arabella?"

"Good God, no! I'll have you know I do not hold with making a great fuss over nothing. Just call my maid and she will make me a hot chocolate. I shall be right as a trivet directly. Don't need no sawbones, either."

He looked ruefully at his aunt and a smile broke over his features. She was a strong old lady and he was proud of her spirit.

"You will of course see the doctor if only to set my mind at rest. I cannot have my favourite aunt collapsing for want of care."

"I am not a ninny-hammer, Sebastian. I have suffered worst hurts than this, I can tell you."

"And tomorrow, dear Aunt you may tell me about all these hurts you have suffered because I do want to hear of them, but not at the present moment. I need to go and discover where Darcy is and why he was in this corridor at one of the clock in the morning."

"Harris has gone after him. He seems like an able bodied fellow."

"He is Aunt, never fear on that score," and with that he carried his aunt back into her room much to that lady's displeasure and gently lowered her on to her bed. Only when her maid was with her and she had settled did he go in search of Darcy.

Much to his surprise, Darcy was not in his room. His bed was still turned down in preparation for the night and when questioned, his valet had not seen him. He had been dozing in a chair waiting for his Lordship's arrival.

The duke frowned.

Please don't let my earlier suspicions be true!

After a thorough search of the Hall he was much intrigued and relieved to find him in the Library slouched on a chair, an empty bottle of port lying at his feet, out for the count.

The duke was even more surprised to discover Jonas Althrop lounging in another chair opposite, finishing off a decanter, bleary eyed with a smug smile on his face.

"I thsay, dook, it hain't a bad port, you got yourshelf ere."

"Only to glad to accommodate you, Althrop! If you will excuse me, I have something to see to," and with that he strolled out of the room content to believe that his cousin had no part in tonight's activities. Moreover, he now believed that the perpetrator of tonight's work was a family member. He was convinced it was someone remotely connected that looked similar enough to Darcy and who could pass himself off as him.

He had to find Harris, but where to begin looking. First, he would check on his aunt and Arabella. He could take no chances with his family. After posting men outside the library, outside his aunt and Hettie's apartments and Arabella's, he gathered a few more to assist him in his search for Harris.

This took a while as it was a dark night, but he was eventually discovered between the house and the lake knocked out cold. A few men carried him back to the Hall and he was placed in the drawing room on a couch, while they waited patiently for the doctor. Unfortunately, he failed to make an appearance that night.

By the time breakfast was over the next morning, everyone was apprised of the events of the night before. The bleary eyed, Darcy, was much shocked and a sense of gravity pervaded the room. Dismissing the servants, the duke looked at each person then made a decision to tell all that he knew. It was the only way now that he could justify the heavy guard placed around the Hall both inside and out.

As he related the details, all agreed that the man had to be a madman to make another attempt to break in but they also decided between them that he had to be crazy to murder so many people. "Of course, we could still be wrong in our suppositions, but I cannot take chances with people's lives.

"Sir Edgerton is on his way and I hope you will understand the need for cooperation when he asks questions. It is imperative that we get to the bottom of this."

"Even more so when Lady Peabody thinks she recognises me as a person who could harm her," Darcy stated peevishly. He had resented the summons to the breakfast room after a heavy night of drowning his sorrows over one particular lady. Althrop, coming down for a book, had decided to join him and they had both spent a couple of hours commiserating with one another over ladies well out of their reach.

Darcy was surprised and angry to hear the news that Lady Peabody had been injured and that she had thought him capable of such a thing.

"What was I to think, dear boy? The man was the image of you."

"How is Harris?" Arabella asked promptly, wishing to prevent an argument between Darcy and her aunt. She would need to do something about Hettie as well who was whimpering quietly in the corner with Reverend Althrop trying to calm her frayed nerves. The revelation that her dear Constance had suffered an attack and a burly man knocked unconscious had come as a tremendous shock to her nerves. Now, the knowledge of the threat to the duke had quite overset her.

"He is still unconscious but the doctor is returning, shortly. He has nasty bruising and a bump on his head but we do not think any bones are broken."

After a few minutes, Sir Edgerton arrived with more news. He explained that another man had been discovered in the woods, shot through the heart at point blank. This was too much for Hettie, who was eventually persuaded to retire to her room and promised a sedative when the doctor arrived. The reverend kindly offered to escort her and ensure that a sturdy guard was placed on her door.

Returning to the drawing room, he took his turn in answering questions but could not tell them anything of value as he had been well under the influence of a good port while all the shenanigans were going on. Sir Edgerton was interested in Darcy's resemblance to the culprit and even more interested in the diary that the duke felt it incumbent to pass over to him even though it would once again, allow others to know of his first wife's betrayal.

He comforted himself in the knowledge that if it helped to save lives, it had to be done. Once Sir Edgerton had questioned everyone he took his leave. They were left to ponder the events until the doctor arrived and almost in the same instant, the duke's lawyer. After a few words with the doctor and a promise that he would not leave until he had talked to him, the duke and Darcy excused themselves to go to the study.

Arabella had wished to accompany them but a silent shake of the head from her husband kept her in her seat. Her place was with her aunt who even though she would not admit it, was shaken up by all that had happened. If Arabella was truthful, she herself, did not know how much more she could take.

They were virtual prisoners in the Hall surrounded by guards and even though she knew the reason why, she resented being a victim to this evil man who had robbed everyone's happiness in an attempt to become duke.

For Arabella was certain that that was what he was after. A mad man who thought he had a right to the dukedom. The problem was, they were working in the dark as they knew nothing about him, except that he had the look of Darcy.

The doctor examined Lady Peabody and pronounced her to be fit. His suggestion that she rest quietly for a while to overcome the shock she had sustained fell on deaf ears. He prescribed laudanum in case she found difficulty sleeping and promised a sedative for Lady Henrietta which would see her feeling much better directly.

It was then the turn of Harris, who unfortunately had sustained a masterful blow to the head and was still unconscious. The old doctor shook his head and explained that in his experience, head injuries of this nature were very dangerous and he could not be sure of the outcome.

"I will go and report to the duke but do not hesitate to call me if there is any change in his condition."

Arabella had the servants carefully remove him to a bedroom where he could hopefully recover in both comfort and safety. She also ordered a guard to be placed in front of his door and someone to sit with him both day and night. The staff would need to take it in turns to watch over him. She felt because Harris could probably identify the culprit once he regained consciousness, his life would be in danger.

"For forgive me Aunt but I cannot quite feel that either of you are safe from this fiend. I fear that he will believe you or Harris could identify him so we must be vigilant at all times."

"Yes my love, for we do not know the workings of a mind such as his."

After luncheon they both decided to retire to their rooms for a much needed rest after all the shocks of the day. Althrop, however, chose to take a book from the library to pass the time until the dinner bell.

****

"So, you think this could be our man, Lewis?"

The elderly lawyer considered the duke's words.

"Indeed, I do, your Grace. It is quite possible." Lewis continued to describe the man they believed may be responsible. He resides on the fringes of polite society, calling himself a gentleman. A veritable card sharp, he has made enormous sums and dresses as fine as any gentleman of the ton."

Darcy was not completely convinced. "So, in your estimation, this is our man?" He couldn't for the life of him see a connection from what they had been told.

"Fortunes are won and lost as you know and this Jeremiah won an extensive estate off Lord Bracken about six years ago.

The poor gentleman blew his brains out and on the same day, this Jeremiah Blackstock evicted his family. It was lucky for them that they could go for shelter to another family member.

"I remember that." Darcy said. "Good God, man, his estate borders mine and is close to yours, Cuz. Do you think he targeted Bracken on purpose?"

The duke also looked much shocked. "Do you think he cheated him out of the estate?"

"There was much talk of it but nothing could be proved."

"I still don't understand what this has to do with us." The duke stated, now completely perplexed.

"Well Cuz, if this is our man, he certainly has no conscience. To throw a mother and four children out of their home and take up residence himself? The man is certainly no gentleman!"

"I think I ought to tell you something of his past." The lawyer said.

"I have never disclosed this information because it was the wish of your uncle to keep it a secret, but now that lives are at risk, I think I should break my silence."

The duke poured them all a stiff brandy and they sat down before the lawyer related the information he was reluctant to give. After a few moments, he told the tale.

"It was a long time ago of course but your Uncle Arnold fell in love with a totally unsuitable girl. In fact she was a servant in your grandfather's house. The girl discovered she was with child so was paid off and a sum of money settled on her and the infant for the rest of their lives."

"He didn't marry her did he?" The duke wondered why he had never had wind of this. Often, stories passed down within the family circle, but this appeared to be hushed up so that no-one else knew. Strange, he thought.

"No, no, your Grace. He knew what he owed the family. He joined the army as you know and fell at the Battle of Aboukir in 1801."

"Yes, we knew about that, but what has this to do with our man?"

"About six years ago, he came to me demanding more money and waving a wedding certificate in front of my nose telling me he was the rightful heir to Arnold's fortune. Of course it was false, but I had it checked out just in case. He was quite persistent telling me I should treat him with the respect he deserved as the grandson of a duke.

It was then that I told him that he was not a gentleman but an illegitimate son of a man who at the time was far too young to know his own mind. It was then that he became angry and cursed the whole house of Winslow, saying they would all pay for the crimes against him. I thought him quite mad at the time and had him thrown out. It is not until now that things are beginning to add up and after hearing of the recent events, I think there is every likelihood that he committed all these atrocities."

"I agree," the duke replied. Everything appeared to be falling into place at last. He now believed that he had a name and an address of the person who had caused such havoc in his life over the last few years. He could call the magistrates and have the man arrested as soon as he entered Bracken's estate. The sense of relief he felt showed on his face.

"Hold on, Seb," Darcy said, putting his hand up as if to stop him in mid tracks, "we still have no concrete evidence. Admitted, everything points to him but until Harris regains consciousness, we have no-one to identify him as the person in the Hall last night."

"I'm afraid that is true, your Grace. You need evidence to have him arrested. I will say, his resemblance to Lord Rutherford is startling, however."

"You see! We must wait for Harris to regain consciousness."

"If he regains consciousness, you mean." The duke replied. "Until then, we must remain vigilant and hope that he doesn't kill anyone else."

Chapter Fourteen

Two weeks passed by without incident, except for Harris's improvement. He had regained consciousness after three full days and though at first, very weak, grew stronger every day.

The only problem was that he could not remember anything about the incident. When the doctor was again summoned, he advised them that this was a common occurrence after a nasty knock on the head.

"In some cases, a person remembers in time, but many never regain their memory."

Both the duke and Darcy were frustrated by this news but resigned themselves to the search for Blackstock. The duke had sent men to Bracken's estate to keep watch for him in the off chance that the man should return there. His men were still patrolling the perimeter of the estate to ensure that no-one entered the Hall who were not welcome. For now, all they could do was wait patiently for something to happen and be prepared for it when it did.

Meanwhile, Arabella was experiencing nausea regularly in the mornings and had accepted the fact that she was more than likely carrying Sebastian's child. She was elated at the thought but didn't wish to say anything until the doctor confirmed it.

She hoped Sebastian would feel as pleased as she did and couldn't wait to inform him. The doctor was visiting her today so she would not have long to wait for the news. The only sadness was that the duke would not have any reason to sleep with her as she reluctantly reminded herself theirs was a marriage of convenience. The thought upset her, but pride came to the fore.

She would wait for the doctor to confirm her pregnancy then deal with the situation afterwards. The hours ticked around until mid-day when the doctor entered the room.

He didn't take long to examine her and congratulated her on her forthcoming child. She beamed at him as he was ushered out of the bedroom. Feeling incredibly happy, she had Molly dress her hair and chose her prettiest orange, silk morning gown to tell him the good news.

She found him in his study signing papers, for once completely alone.

"May I have a few words with you, Sebastian?" He stood up and smiled in welcome, holding a chair out for her as she sat down and thanked him.

"You look exceedingly pleased with yourself, my love. And by the by, felicitations to you on your birthday. We are having a special dinner this evening to celebrate."

His eyes surveyed the radiant look upon her face. His groin grew painfully aware of her presence and the thought crossed his mind to take her right now over the desk. Unaware of his thoughts, but suddenly noticing the twinkle in his eye, she looked up into his dear face and said,

"Thank you, Sebastian. I will look forward to it." She was touched that he had remembered the date. With so much excitement, she had completely forgotten the date.

"Oh Sebastian, I am extraordinarily pleased with myself at this particular moment and I hope you will be as well with the news." She could hardly contain her emotions.

"Try me!" He said noticing a wonderful glow about her.

"I have just seen the doctor and he has confirmed my pregnancy." Beaming up at him she leaned forward. "I hope you are as pleased as I am."

A look of complete happiness spread over his face. Was that tenderness she saw?

He is probably thinking of the child to come.

"That is wonderful news! I could not be more pleased."

He stood, walking around the desk and lounged against it, pulling her up gently to kiss her tenderly.

"I thought you would be. It does make our marriage worthwhile, doesn't it?"

"Of course. I remember you saying how much you would love to have children, but I must warn you that twins run in our family." His eyes twinkled like stars.

"That would be beyond everything!"

"Yes, but you must take extra care of yourself, Arabella." He gently settled her back into the chair while he resumed his seat on the edge of the desk.

"I promise that I will do everything I can to take care of myself. A baby means too much to me to neglect myself."

"Thank you, Arabella. You do not know how happy that makes me to hear it." He sounded so sincere. She knew she had pleased him.

"Yes, and you Sebastian will have a rest from me as well which I am sure you will be grateful for. It must have been difficult for you to bed a complete stranger when your heart was not involved."

Sebastian's face turned wooden.

"Was it difficult for you, Arabella?" He asked in a strangled voice, dreading the answer. "Forgive me but I thought you enjoyed our love making."

"Oh, I did, but as ours is a marriage of convenience and I have done my duty, you will not need to visit me until after the birth. I quite understand and indeed expect it."

"Do you Arabella, and what about my needs as a man? They do not go away just because you are pregnant. May I not visit you if I have need of your luscious body?"

He moved closer to her, wishing to lay her on the carpet now and take what was his by rights of the marriage certificate. He did not think he could go seven days without her let alone several months.

Arabella thought of those months ahead and dreaded Sebastian seeing her as she grew large with child. It would certainly turn him off her for good. She could not endure that. Sebastian had always made her feel beautiful. He was the only man that ever had.

"Oh I think it would be better if you didn't visit me." She took a deep breath, hoping he would understand. "After all, I will need my rest now you see." She was unable to read what he was thinking and started to feel decidedly uncomfortable.

"And what of your needs, Arabella?" he said hesitantly, "Will you miss me in your bed?"

Of course I will, I will ache for you, but you must not see me when I am big with your child. You will surely turn against me.

"I am sure I can manage to do without your company until after the baby is born. Perhaps after a few weeks of its birth, we can resume relations. I do so very much wish for a large family."

"If that is your last word on it then I will respect your wishes" he said in a dry tone. "If you should change your mind, I am here."

"Thank you, Sebastian. I will remember that." She left the room feeling far less elated than the moment when she had entered.

Sebastian sat at his desk for a long time. A heavy sigh escaped him. He only had himself to blame. He had not bothered to woo her in any way. She didn't even have the jewellery that was hers by right. It was still in the safe locked away.

He had managed everything badly, too worried about the future of the Duchy to take the time to show her the attention she deserved. Why, even Darcy noticed the clothes she wore whereas he would stare into her beautiful, large, almond eyes and merely drown in their depths. Had he ever paid her a compliment? For shame, he did not know. God he was an unromantic soul and deserved her disinterest. He thought of all the times he had wanted to tell her that he had fallen hopelessly in love with her but lacked the courage to do so.

I was scared of her rejection, yet she is nothing like Dulcie. What a coward I am.

He knew he needed to change his ways and become more affectionate towards her, instead of continually holding himself back. She would need all his love and attention now, especially when she grew big with his child. He vowed that he would make her feel the beautiful woman she was; now and for the rest of their lives together.

Arabella reclined in her room with tears running down her cheeks. She would miss his body next to hers. She would miss his closeness, his kisses. She would miss everything about him. How miserable she felt!
She was torn. With all her heart she knew she wanted children, but the thought of spending lonely nights without him filled her with trepidation. She loved him and needed to have him close but the fear that he would turn from her as the baby grew inside her was inescapable. If he had loved her it would have been different. But he didn't.

For years, she had listened to her father yelling terrible words at her, instilling a feeling of inadequacy. He had told her she was useless and had nothing to recommend herself to any man for so long, that finally, she was convinced she had nothing of worth to offer anyone.

When she had looked in the mirror, her image showed a brown haired, slip of a girl that lacked the vivacity of her friends. If she was honest that was why she had believed that no one could love her and had resigned herself to a marriage of convenience.

Then Sebastian came into her life and she couldn't believe it. He was everything she could desire in a man and more. She knew she had jumped at the chance given to her. How lucky she had counted herself. She had felt needed. Unlike her father, Sebastian had listened to her.

But now it would be sheer hell missing his closeness, his love making and his tenderness. Ironically, now she was having his baby, she felt closer to him yet would now need to keep him away. Her bed would be a lonely place full of idyllic memories.

A fresh bout of crying ensued. Sitting on the chaise longue, staring yet unaware of the beautiful view from her bedroom window, she didn't remember a time when she felt this miserable in her whole life.

It was there that Molly found her when she came to dress her for dinner. Arabella had cried herself to sleep.

"My lady," Molly said, "It is time to prepare for dinner. Shall I put the white silk out for you? It is a special occasion after all."

"Oh, Yes Molly, thank you. I must have been tired."

"It is natural, my lady, you will find you are more tired and your emotions will be everywhere at the moment."

"Will they, Molly?" I feel quite tearful, but earlier, I was elated." She stood up and after stretching, she walked over to the dressing table and looked in the mirror. "Perhaps I will just have a tray, Molly."

"But everyone is waiting to congratulate you, my lady. They are all so pleased to hear the news. Mrs Hobbs says that she has never seen his Grace look so happy in years."

Arabella gave a watery smile. "Really Molly, is that what she said?"

"Why yes, my lady. Everyone is so excited about the new baby. It will do you good to go down to dinner. It is bound to raise your spirits After all, it is your birthday."

Arabella looked doubtfully at the mirror. Her face still showed signs of her recent tears.

"We can repair that in a trice." Molly said completely confident of the outcome.

"Very well, do your magic, Molly." She must pull herself together and not dwell on things that couldn't be helped. Molly was right. She needed people around her.

Afterwards, Arabella was glad that she agreed to go down. Dinner was a happy affair and later, while the men were drinking their port and the women took their tea in the drawing room, both her Aunt and Hetty were full of plans for the baby's layette.

The evenings were still somewhat cold, and when the men strolled in Althrop decided he would like to walk in the garden for a while.

"I think I will fetch a warmer coat, though."

"I will walk up with you, if you can wait for me. I am feeling a little tired." Arabella attempted to stifle a yawn. "No, please don't get up. I just hope you can all excuse me. It is the excitement of the day."
Studying her face, Sebastian realised that she did indeed look tired and smiled warmly at her. Ignoring her suggestion that he should stay where he was, he caught her by the elbow. Turning to the rest of the company, he said,

"Excuse me for a moment, I will just see my wife settled." To her surprise, he guided her out of the door and escorted her up to her room.

"You look really tired, my love," he said. "Do you wish me to send everyone away so you may rest?"

She looked into eyes full of tenderness, so much so, she was in danger of crying once more.

"Oh, please don't, Sebastian. It is just that I am a little exhausted today. I will be right as a trivet tomorrow. Well, by lunchtime, anyhow."

"Oh my poor love. Are you nauseous in the mornings? I did not realise as I have been up well before you the last couple of weeks."

How attentive he was! She loved this side of him. He made her feel cared for.

"Just a little, Sebastian, but I am quite myself normally by the time luncheon is here and often ravenous."

He kissed her gently, a whisper of a kiss over her lips that made her insides tremble. Then he kissed her again, gathering her into his arms.

"Goodnight, my love." He whispered into her mouth, and opened the door behind her. "Tomorrow morning I will send Mrs Hobbs to you with some dry toast. She used to swear by it if I remember rightly. Shall I tell Molly to come to you?"

"No, I have given her the night off. She is walking out with one of the footman so I thought I could do without her tonight."

"Are you sure?"

"Yes, I'm fine. Goodnight, Sebastian. Thank you." Arabella replied, smiling up at him.

She walked through the door and closed it behind her, leaning her back against it, still feeling the imprint of his mouth against hers.

"Touching!" A husky voice said, coming from the corner of the room. Arabella froze with fear for a moment. She knew who this man was. He walked towards her with a sneer on his face. She had seen him before and would never forget his leering gaze. This was the man who Sebastian saved her from all those years ago at the Muchbury Ball. She would never forget a face that emanated such evil.
"What are you doing here?" She tried not to allow her voice to tremble.

"The diary. I have come for the diary," he said walking up to her and standing too close. She could feel his breath on her face and tried to move her head away to no avail.

"I do not have it!" He searched her face and decided she was sincere.

"No, I don't think you do. So it must be in Sebastian's hands. He's a dead man."

Arabella trembled.

Dear God, I can't scream because he might hit me and that could hurt my baby. What am I to do?

Suddenly, he grabbed her and a rag was placed over her nose. She could hardly breathe. She tried to struggle but he was too strong and soon she knew no more.

Chapter Fifteen

"Too much excitement for one day." Lady Peabody declared. She needs her rest."

"Yes Aunt, I will make sure she is not disturbed. He had to admit that Arabella looked quite strained this evening even though she had smiled and conversed quite animatedly at times.

He could tell something was bothering her and he believed she had attempted to hide the fact that she had been crying, earlier.

Tomorrow, he would give her the sapphires and tell her of his love for her. He would hope that one day she would feel the same but would not press her. History had taught him that one couldn't make people feel the way that you would like. He would be patient. For now, what he had was enough. It had to be.

Lady Peabody and Hettie decided to have an early night and were just making their way to the door when Althrop came strolling in.

"I say Lord Rutherford, what were you taking to the Duchess Suite earlier? I thought that was out of bounds to us all!"

"When was that?" Darcy said suddenly alert, looking at Sebastian meaningfully.

"Why, not forty minutes ago. Just before I went out. Well perhaps it was about an hour ago. You needn't deny it. I saw you just as you entered, carrying a sack. What an earth did you have in there. Looked mighty heavy."

Both Sebastian and Darcy dashed passed Althrop, almost knocking Lady Peabody over in their efforts to pass through the doorway.

They ran up the stairs, two at a time in their haste to reach the Duchess Suite. As they entered, they found it in darkness so fumbled around for tinder and candles to light the room.

As soon as light permeated the room, they discovered Simms, lying on the floor, a knife in his chest.

"Dead! Dear God, how many more? The man is a maniac." Sebastian sighed, frustrated by the cold blooded killer. "Ask Danvers to send someone for Edgerton and best call the doctor. The women will need him even if this poor man won't."

"How did he get passed the men?" Darcy asked.

"He must have come up the passage way. Could have thrown this knife, we will never know. Obviously looking for the diary because look at the drawers and cupboards. He has had a thorough search."

"And not discovering it here, he may have gone up to the attics. I would put nothing passed him. Let's go have a look." Darcy stated.

"Take someone up with you, don't go alone, while I go check on my wife. I will just pop my head through the door to make sure she is asleep. I do not wish to disturb her but I'll put someone on the outside of it this evening so if she is disturbed by any noise they can let me know right away."

Darcy looked curiously at him.

"I have decided to let her rest, Darcy. She is fagged to death so I will not disturb her tonight unnecessarily. I certainly don't want her becoming upset about this night's work."

Darcy nodded in understanding. "I'll fetch one of the men and we'll explore the attics. Best to leave everything as we find it here for Edgerton. Blackstock has long gone by now."

Sebastian walked towards his wife's door and popped his head around. As he expected, the room was in darkness, but he could just make out his wife's outline in the bed. She did not move, so he was determined not to have her disturbed. He closed the door, quietly and crept away.

At least she would be undisturbed by this night's work. Now, if his Aunt had not retired, he would have to explain what had happened.

Thank God Hettie has retired!

****

Sebastian and Darcy were up early the following morning, in preparation for the visit from Edgerton and the doctor. Both were unable to show the previous evening; Edgerton pleaded an important dinner party and the doctor was called away to a difficult labour.

The two men were not in the slightest surprised to receive Edgerton just as they were finishing their breakfast. After greeting him, they took him up to the Duchess Suite where he asked many questions and looked around for signs of a scuffle.

"It looks to me as though, Simms heard a noise from behind the panel and went forward to investigate," Edgerton explained as he surveyed the scene before him.

"I would judge that as the panel opened the killer stabbed him, taking him by surprise." He walked closer to the panel then said, "If you look here, it looks as though the gun Simms was holding dropped to the floor. It seems that the killer had the element of surprise."

"We thought he may have thrown the knife," Darcy suggested.

"No, I do believe, he staggered back from the savage way he was attacked. This man acts first and thinks afterwards. I would think he is quite a desperate character."

Just then, Mrs Hobbs came to the door but would not enter. "If you please, your Grace." She looked worried but the duke could not blame her with all the problems besetting them at present.

"A word with you your Grace."

The duke frowned then he strode towards Mrs Hobbs.

"What is it, Mrs Hobbs?" He asked feeling a sick roiling in his stomach. "Is anything wrong with the Duchess?"

"We hope not, your Grace. Molly and I have just gone to her suite but she is gone."

Mrs Hobbs continued looking very scared.

"Her bed was not slept in. A pillow was placed long ways so that one would think she slept, but when we neared the bed, there was no one there and her night rail has not been used."

The duke's face was ashen. "I don't understand, she was there last evening. I saw her to the door, then she entered and said she was going to retire for the night."

Sebastian was trying to make sense of it. She would not run away. She would not leave him. Admittedly, she looked strained last evening, but he couldn't believe that she would just go.

No, she had been happy. She had accepted my kisses and smiled tenderly at me. She likes me, I know. She would not leave me. Please God, don't let her leave me. I could not stand to lose her now!

He would not withstand the pain if he had lost her.

"What's wrong?" Darcy asked.

"Has the duchess taken ill? I'll ride for the doctor and drag him here by his neck if so."

The duke turned to him, his face like death.

"She's gone, Darcy. She's left me."

"Impossible! She would not do such a thing. I have seen how she looks at you."

"That will be all, Mrs Hobbs. Please go to the duchess's room and have Molly look to see what she has taken with her."

"Yes, your Grace, I am sure there is a simple explanation. I will have the house searched in case she has fallen asleep somewhere else." Mrs Hobbs curtseyed then walked hurriedly away.

Sebastian's face took on hope at Mrs Hobbs' words, then his face fell as he remembered their conversation the day before.

"It was only yesterday, Darcy that she reminded me that ours was a marriage of convenience and she denied me her bed until after the child is born. Does that sound like someone who cares for another?"

Surprise and disbelief crept over Darcy's face.

"No, I cannot believe that."

"Nevertheless, it is true."

"So that is why you didn't stay with her last night?"

"That, Darcy, was because she was fagged. I would not have let matters lie that way for good. I was just giving her a little time, that's all."

They walked downstairs to the study in silence. Crossing to the mahogany, side table, the duke poured them a brandy

He could not rest. He paced the floor, trying to think of reasons why she might take flight.

"Doesn't she realise there is a murderer on the loose who would not think twice of killing her?" He was becoming angry and took some deep breaths in an attempt to calm himself.

A knock on the door disturbed his melancholy. Darcy walked over and ushered Edgerton in.

"Your Grace, I will need to see the rest of the household. Someone may have seen something last night that would help us with our enquiries."

"God damn you, we know who did it! It was Blackstock!" He barked, still striding backwards and forwards like a man possessed. "You would do more good finding the bastard!" he roared, "My wife is out there somewhere and she will be a sitting target for him."

God how am I going to live without her?

"Tell me, your Grace, at what time did your wife go missing?"

"I don't know! I said goodnight to her about nine of the clock last evening. I haven't seen her since. When I checked her at about ten of the clock, for all intents and purposes, she appeared to be there; but I cannot even swear to that you see as I merely looked through the door and saw what I thought was her shape in the bed fast asleep."

"So she could have left much earlier?" Edgerton asked calmly.

"I do not know. I'm sorry Edgerton, forgive me for my manners. This business has overset me somewhat. You see, my wife is with child and I fear for her safety."

"I do understand, your Grace. If you will allow it, I will question everyone and see what I may discover. You will not be going anywhere in the next couple of hours, will you?"

"Hardly, my wife might be found and I wish to be here to ensure her safety. I have failed to look after her but that will be rectified as soon as we discover where she is."

"Then by your leave, I will see what I can unearth and come back to you as soon as I have finished my enquiries."

"Thank you Sir Edgerton, we will be here." Darcy answered as he poured them both another brandy.

He walked over to Sebastian and handed him the glass.

"Here, take this. I think you need it." He retrieved the other glass from Seb's loose fingers and closed them back around the full one. Sebastian allowed him to do so, looking dazed.

"Thanks, Darcy," he replied.

"God you do not know how I feel at this moment." He emptied the tumbler and strode to the window, "She is out there somewhere and I don't know where to begin looking for her."

"That's where you are wrong, Seb, I do know how you feel. I've been there; still am I suppose. Numb though. I am in the same boat as you in many respects. Only I don't envisage mine coming back to me."

"You never talk about it."

"I can't! It's too raw. One day perhaps, but not yet."

"Come sit, we will drown our sorrows while others try to discover what's going on. I am good at that. In fact, I am the best. Everything is always given to me on a plate."

"Yes Seb, you can feel sorry for yourself for that, while there are others who starve in this world. Poor you!"

"Oh to hell with you! Make yourself useful and pour the brandy."

Darcy walked over to the table then paused. A fearful thought suddenly hit him and he glanced reluctantly at Seb wondering how he would respond to his suggestion.

"I say Seb, you don't think that this Jeremiah fellow has taken the duchess, do you?" Fear laced itself into Sebastian's features.

What if that was true. I could not bear it!

Sebastian took a deep breath.

"He could not have passed the men with the duchess. She would never have gone willingly.

Please, not that!

Chapter Sixteen

Arabella's head throbbed and she retched. She was thirsty but at the moment she was still alive.

Please God, don't let me die. I have never told him how much I love him. I am carrying a child. Please don't let me die.

In the dim light, she could make out the man who had drugged and abducted her. From a distance, he looked the image of Darcy. She was shocked by the similarity.

At the moment, he slept, snoring loudly. He must have thought that she would sleep longer because at least he had not gagged her. She looked again at his face in repose.

No wonder everyone thought you were him. But up close, you have an evil face; a killer's face. God, how could Dulcie have lain with you? She had to be out of her mind.

He stirred and she almost jumped out of her skin. Where was she? Where had he brought her? She listened for sounds.

The birds were singing. She could hear water. Ducks! Were they near the lake or had he taken her further away. It didn't make sense to keep her so close to the Hall unless he was setting a trap for Sebastian. Surely, they would be discovered here.

Looking around, she discovered a seat with a table covered in a white cloth. There were flowers on the table. Had he placed these items there? Was this the place he had been hiding? It seemed so. He must have prepared this place in readiness for her abduction. Oh God, what was going to happen to her. She was in the same room as a lunatic. Taking deep breaths, she strived for calmness.

They would find her missing and realise he had taken her. Then they would search the property. She tried to move but her hands were tied and it hurt to chafe against her bindings. Looking up, she saw a window. Although it was about waist height, she could see nothing out of it as it was dirty. Just shapes moving. She thought they might be trees.

He stirred again. Then he was awake and leering at her. *God, I feel sick!*

"You're quite a tasty mite! Not like the Lady Dulcie! Different, but fetching." He sat ogling her. She watched him as his eyes scanned her body and her heart beat quickened in fear.

Please God, don't let him touch me! I couldn't bear it !

"Are you hungry?"

She shook her head from side to side, slowly.

"That's what I like! A woman who knows when to keep her mouth shut. You see, women don't listen. They talk too much. Dulcie did, Briany did. Look what happened to them!"

She stared at him, trying to keep her face neutral.

"I can see you are a good listener." He moved a little closer to her.

"A gentleman now……….. he needs a good listener. Perhaps I wouldn't have needed to kill so many people if they had listened to me. But no! They turned their backs as though I was nothing." An ugly scowl appeared on his face and he looked at her with murder in his eyes.

She shook with fear not knowing what this man was going to do with her and feeling so helpless.
At the moment, he appeared to be deep in thought.

Jeremiah looked at the young woman. He might take her in a moment. He could do with a woman and this one was different to the ones he normally bedded. Looking out of the grimy window, he checked to see if anyone was around. No, no-one here. Good.

He continued to look out of the dirty window, while his mind roamed back to a time when he was a small child. He'd listened to his mother, telling him how brave his father was. That great man had fought in the army and was a gentleman. His father had bought them the house that they lived in and twice, he had visited.

He remembered his mother saying,

"And you will be a great gentleman one day. Just like your father. He has given me money, you see, for your future.

He remembered one of the occasions his father had visited him. He had asked if he could go with him. He had turned to him and smiled, but he had not answered him. He had not listened to him. Nobody did.

"You will listen though." He said moving closer to her. "You will listen to me."

She nodded, now petrified of this man whom she felt could kill again at any time.

"I had to have them killed. It was the only way to revenge myself. They turned their backs on my mother. She wasn't one of them. Too good for the likes of her. My father didn't marry her, you see." His face took on another scowl.

"He was the son of a duke. She was a maid in the big house. She died, when I was fourteen of a broken heart. They killed her with their snobbery. I didn't know what to do. The parish helped me bury her, then I was on my own."

Arabella listened, knowing that a son of a duke could never marry a servant. But he had visited her even though he couldn't marry her. He must have loved her, she thought.

"I used to watch the three boys as they grew up. They were much the same age as me. Perhaps I was slightly older. Two brothers, one cousin. All growing up together. They went to Eton. I went to the parish school, yet we shared the same grandfather."

He shifted his position and glared at Arabella. She didn't move. It was as if he was in his own world.

"When I was older, I went to the lawyers and asked for what was mine by right. My father had been killed yet I could not inherit. Still the outsider. The lawyer said I was no gentleman, but I showed him."

He suddenly realised where he was.

From a flask, he poured an amber liquid into a cup and pushed it towards her lips. She urged at the smell of it.

"You don't like brandy?"

"Just some water, if you please, Sir." It would be better to remain humble in this man's presence.

He laughed. "Water it is," and slopped some into a dirty container and pushed it into her mouth.

"Ppplease," she whispered, "Untie my hands," I am feeling so ill." And with that she retched again.

He looked down at her with disgust in his eyes.

"Not the fine lady now, are you, eh?" He moved close to her ear. She couldn't help herself trembling.

"Retch away. I will not untie you. Do you think I am stupid. I know your type. You think you will get away, but you won't. I am waiting for him to come and then I will kill him and his heir. Then I will be duke."

Arabella remained silent. He still desired the dukedom but he would never attain his dream because the man was illegitimate. He truly believed in his claim. He was mad.

He walked towards the door, then turned towards her. "Now Andrew…. The heir to a dukedom and the pride of his father. He was easy, though I didn't expect it to be. All I had to do was shoot my gun in the air as he was about to jump the fence and that was that. He took a fall and the horse fell on top of him."

He smiled to himself, thinking back to that fateful day. "That was good timing, but I'm clever like that."

"I'd just returned from my estate. I won it at cards off a Baron. I have a way of winning you see. Anyway the estate will be an asset to the dukedom when I inherit. See, I have started already. I am increasing the coffers. Let them tell me I am not a gentleman! I have my own estate." He smiled to himself as if enjoying a private joke.

Waving the brandy flask around, he took another sip then once more looked into her frightened eyes. He liked a frightened woman. Far better than the confident bitches that turned their noses up at him. He would scare her a bit more and then he would have her. She would know how powerful he was.

He looked towards her again. "Well, what do you think? Don't you agree?" She nodded her head thinking what an evil man he was.

"I was clever, though! I am a patient man. I can wait for the main prize."

She had difficulty keeping up with what he was saying and where his mind wondered. He seemed to jump from one topic to another and repeat himself. He had gloated over killing poor Andrew. A young man in his prime. He wanted her to hear about his evil doings. She would be forced to listen but she could not bear to hear all the awful details. Yet she knew she had to listen and show him respect. He seemed to respond better to that. She would nod her head in agreement and try to appease him at all costs.

To her dismay, he sat down on the dirty floor next to her and after a few minutes of silence, continued his story.

"I hired a couple of heavies for the Duke and his Duchess. It was a stormy, wet night. The men cut down a tree on the main track that night and so the carriage had to take the cliff path. That was my plan. Good, wasn't it?" She nodded, her insides shaking.

"It was easy for my men to run them off the road and over that steep cliff. They didn't stand a chance. Went straight into the icy waters below."

Oh God, this man was responsible for so many murders! He openly bragged about them as if they weren't human beings at all. Just pawns in his game.

"Lady luck has been on my side. The lady Dulcie was next. She was an aristocratic whore! Not like you. You would never give yourself willingly to a stranger, would you?"

Arabella didn't know what to answer. If she said no, he might take offence and if she said yes, he might also take offence. She opted for saying nothing at all.

"No, I can see it in your eyes. The true lady. Not like the whore. She was insatiable, but you wouldn't know about things like that. Then she turned against me and I knew I had to get rid of her before she ruined everything.

Silly bitch! It was easy to push her down the stairs. I had given her a lethal dose of laudanum first to ensure she wouldn't survive. She didn't know. She thought she was drinking brandy. Stupid fool! I did Sebastian a favour that day."

Arabella was blue with the cold and shivered involuntary. Noticing, he pulled a piece of sacking around her shoulders and continued with his story.

"Of course, I have had men attempting to kill both Sebastian and Darcy but the imbeciles have bungled it each time. Best to do the job myself." He took another swig of the bottle of brandy.

"I had Briany on the inside. She was a sexy bitch." Arabella could not prevent a gasp of pure shock.

He laughed. "You are shocked, my little one." He said moving even closer to her. She wanted to pull away from him as he smelled of sweat as though he had not washed for days or even weeks. She had to stop thinking these things or else she would retch again.

"The fine Lady Dulcie didn't know that I planted her maid in the house while she lived in London. I play the long game, you see. I used to take in turns with Dulcie and her and then, Briany became my eyes and ears" He laughed, "Her mistress had no idea."

So Briany had been a traitor from the beginning. Arabella could hardly believe his words. The man was a maniac. He had no conscience at all.

"Jenkins killed her by mistake of course. He mistook her for you. I needed to punish him for that because he nearly wrecked all my plans. Had the cheek to ask me for payment. Nobody fleeces Jeremiah Blackstock."

He fumed for a while, in his own world. She couldn't guess what he was thinking.

"Yes, he met his end at the end of my pistol. His payment it was………….. Justice I say. I shot him through the heart. Bullseye!" He laughed raucously pretending his finger was a gun.

Oh no, he had planned to have me killed as I walked in the woods. Then he killed the man who made a mistake in identity. Of course, Briany used to wear Dulcie's cast off clothes. Those clothes had certainly cost her dearly.

She tried to control her trembling but it was no use. She was petrified of this man and had no way of breaking free from him.

Please, Sebastian, come and save me but don't allow him to kill you. I am so very scared. God forgive me for being such a coward!

He put his arms around her and held her close. She tried not to cringe.
"You see, then I had a problem! I needed to retrieve the diary. I had sent Briany back for it because she could make the excuse of saying sorry and it was only because of her love for her mistress that she had acted as she had. I had thought of that. I am the brains behind it all as you will discover."

She forced a smile onto her face and nodded in agreement. Anything to appease him and keep him sweet. He tightened his hold and she closed her eyes, but he was in a different world to her. The world of what had already transpired.

"I tried once, taking supplies and staying in the Hall in a spare bedroom. I would creep down to the kitchens in the middle of the night. Then guests came."

That would be Althrop, my Aunt and Hettie.

Another wave of shock attacked her

He had actually stayed in the Hall while they slept. How had he achieved this? How did he conceal himself so easily?

"By then, I had searched the attics and the Duchess Suite, but one night, an old lady was in my way and I had to stall her so that I could escape. Then, I had to knock a stupid footman over the head. That was a close call. His men are imbeciles. I will sack them all when I am duke."

Again she nodded her head in agreement with him. If only he would untie her hands.

He smirked, congratulating himself on his achievements. Deep in thought, he laughed a little to himself and then once again, looked at Arabella. She didn't like the sudden change in his eyes that turned from smiling to smouldering. A filthy finger traced the line of her mouth. She tried to keep as still as she could but a gasp escaped her.

"I reckon you could be a passionate little thing. He moved closer and her breathing became fast, her heart pulsating in her chest. Do you like my touch?" He asked as his hands continued down to her breasts and suddenly squeezed.

"Pplease, don't do that. I am frightened." She cried out in terror.

"I can be gentle," he purred. "I am known to be an expert lover and could bring you pleasure beyond your dreams, my lady. But you are wise to be afraid of me."

"I am, Sir!" Arabella was terrified.

"Lord Blackstock! Call me Lord Blackstock! I am the grandson of a duke." He roared, terrifying her more as tears rolled down her cheeks.

"Lord Blackstock," she whimpered.

"Louder, say it louder and with respect." With that, he ripped the front of her gown and he slid his hands into the soft flesh.

"Yes, my Lord Blackstock!" She whimpered, hating his touch but unable to do anything about it.

"You like my touch, girl?" He asked into her mouth.

Please God, help me. He is going to ravish me and I cannot stand it!

His mouth descended painfully on hers wreaking of brandy, while his hands roamed her body at will. She cried, but his mouth did not leave hers. He was rough and he hurt her, but she was totally powerless to do anything to save herself.

He is going to rape me here and now.

"You are a comely little thing. Too good for the likes of the cold duke. Oh yes, I know all about him. You need a man in your bed, my lady." His breath was so close to her cheeks, she felt like retching.

Tears rolled down her face as he lifted her skirts and moved his hands up her legs. She shook from head to toe and could hardly breathe. He took her mouth in his and pushed his tongue into her, devouring her. He was touching her in that private place.

"Oh yes, my Lady, you like my touch there don't you."

"Oh God, please stop!" she begged and wriggled under him which only seemed to inflame him more. He moved over her fumbling with his trousers, then ripped her undergarments clean away.

Oh no, please God, don't let this happen to me. **She cried.**

Suddenly, through her fear, she heard a sharp sound like something heavy suddenly smash against the window.

Jumping up, he straightened his clothes as a stone came hurtling through, smashing the glass.

"Who's there?" He barked. He walked over to the dirty window.

"I'll kill whoever's there and with that he retrieved his pistol and slowly opened the door. A sound had him running outside and shouting some obscenities at whoever he had seen.

She tried to wriggle to straighten her skirts but it was impossible. Her hands were tied and she could do nothing to make herself descent.

Suddenly, he came back through the door, placing his gun in the waistband of his pants. She could hardly breathe. Please don't let him touch me again. I could not bear it!

"My lady," he said, "Pray let's make you presentable. We don't want strangers seeing what is mine."
She was shocked by his tone. His mood had changed, thank God, but what was to come? He straightened her skirts and tried to repair the damage to her bodice, to no avail. Reaching for sacking, he gently placed it over her

to hide her bare breasts that had turned red with his manhandling.

"He will not make you feel like I will make you feel, but you are a lady and he shall not have you. I will make you mine when the time is right. He cannot love you like I will. When he comes, I will kill him and then I will take you for my own."

"But ours is a marriage of convenience. He will not care that I am kidnapped." She said in an effort to save her husband.

"Hmm! Eventually, he will search the boathouse even though he may not have feelings for you."

"I doubt it very much! Indeed, we have no emotional attachment at all," she lied.

"Perhaps then, lady, we might form one. You and me. You are just the type of real lady I like. You have listened to me. Probably the first person in my life that has."

He moved closer and kissed the top of her head. She tried not to cringe at his touch She knew she must play along if she was to save her life and that of the duke's.

"But I will court you properly. You are a lady, after all." He reluctantly moved away after touching her breasts one last time. "In fact, if you can be patient, I will bring you fresh water and later, if you are very good, I will untie your wrists." He placed another kiss upon her forehead and moved a little closer.

"Please, my Lord, could you procure me some fresh water and also some bread if at all possible. I am famished."

He looked into her eyes and something must have convinced him that she was sincere.

"For you, I will go to the moon and back," he said and to Arabella's relief moved to stand up. "I will go to the well and get you some fresh water. Stay here, mind or I will kill you." And with that, he was gone.

Arabella heaved a sigh of relief. The man was insane. What could she do? Her bindings were too tight and there was nothing she could see that could cut them.

The man was volatile and she knew that eventually he would kill her unless she could find a way to save herself. She prayed for help but the minutes ticked away. Where was Sebastian? Did he not care a tiny bit about her or their unborn child?

A few minutes later, the door suddenly opened and little Jem's face appeared, smiling at her.

"My lady, I been skimming stones in the lake and I saw a man coming out of this place. I thought I would take me a look in here. I didn't expect to find you trussed up like this."

"Oh, Jem, I am so glad you are here." She said, "Please, quickly, unloosen this rope so that I can retrieve my derringer."

She was relieved when he did as she asked. Now she would at least have a chance of escape but she knew she must hurry.

"Was it you who hit the boathouse with stones?" Jem looked at her guiltily.

"I didn't mean to. I'm sorry, my lady."

"I am so thankful that you did because a very wicked man was going to hurt me and you saved me from him."

"He chased me but I hid from him. I found a good hiding place."

"Oh Jem, I am so grateful, but you must go for help. Go back to your father and ask him to round up some of the men on the estate."

"No, my lady…….. I cannot leave you here alone. First let me take you to my hiding place, then I will go for help."

"I knows these parts like the back of my hand, my lady. Just you follow me. It is too dangerous for you to go back to the Hall at the moment, but I will run there and get some help, when I knows you are safe."

"Thank you, Jem." She said and hastily followed him out of the boathouse.

Chapter Seventeen

Edgerton sat in the duke's study, having arranged for the body to be taken away. The doctor had called and had pronounced the man dead which by now the whole house knew.

He had also administered a sedative to Hettie who had quite fainted away under the strain of knowing that a man had been murdered under their roof and the duchess kidnapped, because that was what everyone surmised after they had heard Althrop's story.

"We must wait for a ransom note." Edgerton said.

"But we do not know if he has her." The duke said, frustrated at the lack of knowledge.

"Althrop says that the sack he saw the man taking into the Duchess Suite was large and he carried it over his shoulder. It is quite possible that it held the duchess."

The duke's face looked like thunder.

"Would that he told us how large it was last evening when we may have followed him." The duke stated.

"He was not to know at the time that it was a body. Forgive me your Grace, I didn't mean to imply…."

"Enough!" he said and walked to the door.

"Danvers, have my horse saddled immediately and the carriage prepared for her Grace. I am going to find the fiend and when I do, so help me God, I will kill him."

"But your Grace," Edgerton implored hurrying to follow him. "You cannot take the law into your own hands."

"Then do something about it Edgerton, come with me and arrest the fellow."

Sebastian went to the gun room, followed by Darcy and Edgerton who each received a rifle and a pistol.

"Understand your Grace that you could be riding into a trap." Edgerton warned.

"I will take my chances!" He replied and stomped away, oblivious to his visitors and servants who followed his every move.

*****

Blackstock strode into the boathouse, but when he discovered Arabella was missing, he let out a roar of rage. Murder was written all over his face and he vowed he would kill Sebastian and anyone else who had taken her.

He paced up and down the small boathouse smelling her scent and working himself up into a frenzy. He would pay for this. They all would. Nobody would take what was his. He was Lord Blackstock. She had called him by his proper name. The only person ever to do so. He was a grandson of a duke, no less.

She had not laughed in his face like that Dulcie, bitch. She was a lady and she would be his. He moved out of the boathouse, hearing horses hooves coming this way.

"Now I will kill him." He said in a cold voice, the familiar smirk returning to his face.

From her hiding place, Arabella could see and hear clearly what was going on. She would not allow Blackstock to harm Sebastian. Pulling out her derringer, she targeted his knee. She would be ready the instant he raised his pistol.

Sebastian pulled up but remained on his horse. There were seven men altogether, their pistols pointing at Blackstock. He didn't stand a chance, yet the madman was threatening the duke.

"I will kill you, you bastard!" Blackstock warned in a deadly voice. "You have taken her, but she is mine. I have staked my claim."

"You are a dead man if you have touched one hair of her head."

Blackstock laughed.

"Oh I have done far more than that to her but we have unfinished business. She will be mine before the day is out."

Sebastian's face was grim but he realised the man was insane and had little chance of coming out of this alive.

His men would shoot to kill if Blackstock raised his pistol. A movement in the bushes, made him turn, quickly but Blackstock had heard it as well and started to raise his gun towards the sound.

A shot ran out and Blackstock screamed in agony. Arabella had come out of hiding and as soon as he raised his pistol, she fired into his kneecap.

The men dismounted as soon as the shot was fired and they held him fast even though he struggled.

"I will kill you, Sebastian. I will kill you. It is my title, not yours. I am the eldest child." He raged, as the men tied his hands behind his back.

No-one answered him. They were merely relieved that the nightmare was over.

Realising that Sebastian was safe and that Blackstock had been arrested, Arabella fainted clear away.

****

Later, that evening, tucked up in bed after a nice warm bath, Arabella relaxed for the first time in hours. It had been a long day and she had spent a gruelling hour with Sir Edgerton relating the events and the details of Blackstock's past history. Lord Bracken's wife and children would now have their estate restored to them and the duke had decided to do something for Jem's future because they were so grateful for his timely intervention.

Thank you, God, for keeping Sebastian and me safe. She prayed.

It had been hard to face Sebastian after what had transpired with Blackstock and she dreaded telling him the details.

She knew she would need to disclose everything and was fearful that he would turn against her for the terrible things that Blackstock had done to her. Admittedly, he had not entered her private place, but he had placed his hands there, even though there was clothing between them at that time. She shuddered. How close she had come to being completely violated! He had even ripped her undergarments to shreds. Jem had saved her from a fate worse than death just in time.

The door handle turned and she jumped, then realised that it was Sebastian, his face grim, his eyes searching hers.

"Are you feeling better, now?" he asked in a strangled voice.

She searched his face. "Yes, a little, but I seem to be reliving it over and over again and it is driving me to distraction."

"Do you wish to tell me about it?" He asked, dreading what he would hear.

He didn't know if he would be able to contain his anger if the fiend had hurt her and he needed to reassure her no matter what had happened that all would be alright. Sitting down next to her on the bed he pulled her into his arms.

"Now, if you can, tell me what happened, I would wish to hear from the very beginning."

And she did tell him. Every gruesome detail of it. She trembled while she was telling him the worst parts and he stroked and soothed her, trying in vain to take away the fear from her eyes.

"You are safe now, my darling one." He said and gently turned her chin up to kiss her.

"Have you formed a dislike of me, now that I have been violated?" she asked in a strained voice.

He looked shocked.

"I could never form a dislike of you, my love. You were lucky that Jem managed to get there in time, but even if he hadn't, as long as you were returned safely to me is all that matters. I would still love you to distraction. With that, he kissed her hungrily but stopped when he realised that she may not want to be kissed by him, especially after the ordeal she had experienced.

"Did you say that you love me, Sebastian?" She asked, incredulously.

"Yes my love, irrevocably."

The look he bestowed upon her had never seemed so tender. "I thought I had lost you for good and could not bear the pain inside me. It was as though my insides had been ripped away. At first, I thought you had formed a dislike of me as you had earlier reminded me that ours was a marriage of convenience and denied me your bed."

She looked shocked. "But that is only because I was afraid you would turn from me in dislike when I grow big with your child. I would hate that to happen."

He looked into her eyes, sincerity written all over his face.

"Never, my love. You are the most precious person in the world to me. I will be the proudest man when you are big with my child because it is my child you carry."

"Or children!" Arabella reminded him.

"But Sebastian, I never realised it was possible for you to love two women. I always believed that your love for Dulcie would eclipse all others."

His dark eyebrows arched in surprise.

"I did not love, Dulcie. I was dazzled by her in the beginning, but I soon found out her true nature."

"But what about the Duchess Suite? I believed that you loved her so much you could not change it or enter it. Indeed, that is what all the servants believe."

"In the end, I think I disliked her intensely. Or perhaps it was her behaviour. She caused havoc wherever she went. She ridiculed and betrayed me and took a delight when she fed the gossips of the ton. I discovered a dislike for the Season because of her outrageous behaviour, flaunting her lovers for all to see. No, I could not love her. In fact, I do not think I realised what love was until a brunette asked me one day if I could like the idea of a marriage of convenience."

"No, Sebastian, it was you who asked me." She replied, smiling up at him.

A thought struck her. She must find out from him something that had confused her for a number of weeks now.

"Sebastian, why did you always look angry after you made love to me? I believed it was because I was not Dulcie, but if you say that you love me, then what made you turn from me in such a way?"

"It was my fear, my love." He answered,

"The emotions you could arouse in me frightened me to death. I was scared and exceptionally vulnerable when I had buried those feelings for such a long time and you were able to arouse me to such an intensity. I was out of my depth. Once I realised that I loved you, I was able to relax and open up to the wonderful feelings you aroused in me."

"I didn't know!" She snuggled up to him feeling secure in his love.

"It does not matter anymore. Mine is no longer a marriage of convenience. I love you my darling and always will."

"And I love you, Sebastian." She said in a small voice, nestling even closer to him.

"What did you say?" He asked in an incredulous voice, not trusting his ears.

She sat up and looked into his glorious eyes.

"I said, I love you, Sebastian," and proceeded to show him just how much in the nicest way she knew how, much to his Grace's satisfaction.

Epilogue

Almacks was much as he remembered it from the beginning of last year. The dowagers were busily whispering about the latest gossip doing the rounds..

This time, it was about someone other than himself. A smug smile played over his features.

For Sebastian, the major difference was that now he had

a beautiful wife to show off to the world and he would show her off this night to all those present. She had never looked so lovely, in a burgundy, silk dress that clung to her curves .

Her hair was dressed to perfection, piled high on her head and she wore the Winslow sapphires around her neck and on her wrist. Tonight, when they retired to bed, he would give her a set of rubies he had purchased when they had arrived in London yesterday.

He loved showering this woman with presents for she had given him her love and his beloved twin boys a few months ago. The gifts she had bestowed upon him were priceless. He had never believed he could be so happy and didn't care who knew it. Lady Peabody, strolling up to him and tapping him on his arm was quick to say,

"Sebastian, must you make a complete cake of yourself? Don't you know it is unfashionable to hang on your wife's every word for all the world to see?"

Arabella laughed. He looked into her eyes and said,

"But you see, Aunt, I have promised Arabella that I would always be honest with her and so, here you see me, ogling my beautiful wife for all to see."

She beamed at him in approval. "If I were you, I would take her home, early."

"That is my intention, Aunt, never doubt it. She will wish to look in on our sons, anyhow. She will not leave them for long. It is only that we thought to meet Darcy here tonight. As you know, he has given up on his lady love and is looking for a suitable bride. I think he has become so besotted with the twins that he would like to have children of his own."

His wife looked into his eyes and smiled.

"I think it is about time we intervened and assisted him a little, don't you?" she stated, "If you should like it, I will organize a ball and invite all the acceptable debutantes so that he may take his choice amongst them. There has to be someone to replace that woman in his heart."

"Whatever you say, my dear." Sebastian replied, "I would truly like to see him as happy as I am myself."

"My dear Arabella, that is an excellent notion. I will help you." Aunt Constance said, "I think you are going to require my assistance in this. After all, did I not bring you and Sebastian together?"

Once again, Sebastian laughed. "I suppose you did at that."

"Yes dear, you two young ones go home as I can see it is where you would rather be and leave Darcy to me. Tonight, I will make sure that he meets all the right young ladies."

With that, Sebastian and Arabella obeyed their aunt. They both looked forward to a very special night together, knowing that it would be one of many.

If you enjoyed 'Duchess in Danger', follow Darcy's story in 'To love an Earl', coming soon.